WHITE HELL

A TANNER NOVEL - BOOK 17

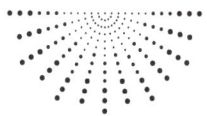

REMINGTON KANE

18 Manhat Hit Man
    Bought

INTRODUCTION

WHITE HELL – A TANNER NOVEL – BOOK 17

Tanner and Sara's small plane crashes into the Siberian wilderness and that's just the beginning of their trouble.

An old enemy of both Tanner and Sara wants them dead, along with a team of mercenaries and dozens of hardened killers.

If that wasn't enough, Tanner must also protect the life of an innocent and deal with a blizzard.

The odds are stacked against them. But this is Tanner, and not even the wilds of Siberia can conquer him.

ACKNOWLEDGMENTS

I write for you.

—Remington Kane

1

NOWHERE TO RUN, NO PLACE TO HIDE

TANNER HAD BEEN LOST IN AN OLD MEMORY WHEN THE trouble began, a pleasant remembrance of childhood.

He was with Sara Blake and flying over the rugged landscape of Siberia in a single-engine plane. But, in his mind, Tanner had been a boy again and traveling with his grandfather, Walter Parker, as the two of them flew above the Delaware mountains of Texas.

HE'D BEEN ONLY TWELVE AT THE TIME AND LOOKING forward to hunting for deer. He'd gone on similar deer hunting trips with both his father and grandfather, but he had been too young to join in the actual hunting. However, on this occasion, he wouldn't just tag along and learn what to do. No, young Cody had paid his dues, had been patient, and would be allowed to participate in the hunt.

Normally, his father would have left Cody's twin sisters, Jill and Jessie, with a family friend who was also one of Cody's teachers, a Mrs. Jennings. The twins were best friends with Mrs. Jennings' daughter, Tonya, but the twins both had the flu. Cody's father had stayed home to care for Jill and Jessie, and yet, he hadn't wanted to cancel the planned hunt, so Cody and his grandfather went on the trip without him.

They were flying on a large ranch in the Texas panhandle that gave hunting tours on its property. The ranch was known for its mule deer, and many a trophy buck had been shot on the land. The twelve-passenger aircraft was loud, but they would only be in the air for a few minutes as they flew up to a higher altitude.

"Are you excited?" his grandfather asked. Walter Parker was a tall, lean man with a weathered, yet still handsome face. He looked younger than his age and had been widowed for over a year, after Cody's grandmother had passed away.

Cody answered his grandfather by smiling and pointing down at the snow-covered landscape. His excitement and joy over the upcoming adventure were plain to see. Although, there was another reason for his smile. She was a girl, and the young blonde was the most beautiful thing Cody had ever seen.

His grandfather saw that Cody had trouble keeping his eyes off the girl, who was on the trip with her mother. Walter Parker had been eyeing the mother. She was blonde as well, mid-forties and, according to the grapevine at the lodge, divorced and available.

"You like that girl, don't you?"

Cody was surprised his interest had been so obvious, but he nodded, that yes, he sure liked the way the girl looked.

"Her name is Genevieve and she's fifteen."

"Fifteen?" Cody said.

"Yep, and that might be a little old for you, seeing as how you're only twelve, but my, she is a beauty."

Cody smiled. "I'm gonna talk to her when we land."

"That's a good idea. You never know, she might have a thing for younger men."

~

"Why the smile?" Sara asked. She had to speak loudly to be heard over the small plane's rumbling engine.

Tanner came out of his memory and pointed at the terrain below, which was thick with trees and coated with a layer of snow, much like the Texas hills had been in his memory.

"I was thinking about a hunting trip I took when I was a boy, and about a girl I met there."

"She must have been pretty if you're still thinking about her."

"My grandfather said she, 'Made grown men wish they were younger and young boys wish they were older.'"

"It sounds like the girl was a knockout," Sara said.

"Oh yeah, and she wanted nothing to do with a twelve-year-old boy, which is what I was back—" Tanner had glanced out the window again as he spoke, and what he saw perplexed him. He looked right, left, then out the plane's small rear window. "We're going the wrong way. I studied a map before the trip. There should be several towns visible, except there's nothing down there but trees."

Their pilot was an amiable older man named Yaromir. They had hired him to fly them to the city of Novosibirsk, from where they'd been staying in Barnaul, Siberia. It was a short plane ride, covering a little more than a hundred miles.

There was a famed zoo in Novosibirsk that had polar

bears and a liger. A liger was the hybrid of a tiger and a lioness. Sara had been looking forward to the trip and was eager to see the polar bears.

"Yaromir, you're going the wrong way," Tanner said.

"I know sir, but I don't have a choice. They said they would hurt my daughter."

Sara didn't speak Russian, so Tanner explained what Yaromir had relayed to him. Afterward, he spoke to the pilot again.

"Who is 'They?'"

"Five large men, all Australian, and an American too, but he was of normal-size, and older."

"Did you get any names?"

"I heard one of the Australians call the American man, Smith."

"What did Smith, look like?"

Yaromir gave a description of Smith that could have fit any number of men, leaving Tanner no closer to knowing who was after him and Sara. However, when Tanner repeated the description to Sara in English, a flash of intuition gave her the answer.

"I'll bet you Smith is Dan Matthews," Sara said. "Matthews speaks Russian and must have fled here to hide from the authorities."

"Where did Smith tell you to take us?" Tanner asked the pilot.

"They said to head south into the wilderness. Once there, I'm to land in the first large clearing I see and wait for them."

Tanner cursed under his breath, looked out the rear window again, and saw what appeared to be a helicopter. It was closing in fast.

Sara saw it too, and she understood what was happening. "They're following us, aren't they?"

"Yeah," Tanner said, then, he spoke to the pilot in Russian. "Yaromir, the men who threatened your daughter are behind us."

"Yes sir, in a helicopter, and I'm so sorry sir, madam. But… maybe they just want to speak with you, da?"

"Land at the first spot you see. They don't want to talk. They're planning on shooting us down."

The old man shook his head in disbelief. "That would be insane."

Tanner stared out the back window once more and saw that the chopper was closer. Although he couldn't be certain, the helicopter appeared to have no door attached on one side. That would be about right if they were planning to shoot at them.

"Yaromir, take us down now. Land in a field, on a frozen lake, anything, but do it now or they'll make us crash."

"What? Oh, hold on, we'll go down in a great rush."

The nose of the plane dipped, and the rest of the small craft followed. Tanner and Sara felt their safety belts tighten as they were made to lean forward. Up ahead was a frozen lake that looked long enough to land on, but the gunfire began when they were still a thousand feet above it.

Yaromir issued forth a prayer in Russian as he fought to land the plane. The chopper flew past while spitting more bullets. Tanner only glimpsed a large blond man who smiled a huge grin. He was holding a semi-auto and firing at them.

Yaromir let out a yelp as blood sprayed the windshield, but the old man stayed with the controls and gave it his best. However, his best wasn't good enough.

The aircraft came down hard on the frozen lake. The plane's propeller took a chunk out of the ice, leaving a hole behind. Then, the craft bounced on its bent wheels. After traveling nearly fifty feet, it came down again and shoved its mangled nose through the ice, and as it did so, Sara screamed in pain.

Tanner had released his seatbelt and covered Sara with his own body when the shooting began, but a piece of the wheel assembly broke through the plane's floor and smashed into her left knee. Thankfully, the metal was blunt, not sharp, but the impact had been great.

"Are you injured?" Tanner asked.

When Sara looked at him, she saw that his left arm was bleeding near the shoulder from a cut caused by a broken window. In the pilot's seat, Yaromir was dead, and his sightless eyes were staring into space.

"I hit my knee on something, but I can walk."

Tanner kicked the door open. "We have to take cover behind the engine block. We'd never make it into the woods before they'd cut us down, and there's nothing but a sheer rock wall the other way."

They tumbled out of the busted plane as, a short distance away, the helicopter touched down on the ice. Five men jumped out and headed their way, while the chopper's pilot stayed with his craft.

As Yaromir said, they were large men. They were also armed with enough firepower to shred what was left of the plane to pieces. The most imposing one was blond and loaded with muscle. Despite the frigid temperature, he was wearing a black sleeveless T-shirt and displayed many tattoos. When he spoke, his voice betrayed his Australian roots.

"Hey over there! Tanner, ain't it? Well, mate, it looks like you've reached the end of the line. You've got nowhere to run and no place to hide, so send out that good-looking sheila and die like a man."

Tanner listened to the man with one ear, literally, as the

other ear was pressed hard against his shoulder. He was straining, as he reached inside a gap that allowed access to the small storage compartment on the belly of the plane. The lower level of the plane was submerged in water. Tanner and Sara were perched on the lip of the jagged hole in the ice that the plane had made after it bounced. They were crouched low and staying behind the engine, as it offered their only cover.

Tanner had removed some of their luggage, but the most important bag was difficult to reach. Its weight caused it to slide back into the far corner of the compartment.

With a grunt of satisfaction, Tanner gripped a handle and removed what he'd been reaching for. It was the bag that held his weapons and ammo. After the zoo trip, they had planned to fly to Moscow on a private jet, then back to the United States, and so their luggage was with them.

"Speak up, mate!" the blond said. "And by the way, my name is Brian. I guess you should know the name of the bloke that's gonna kill ya."

"Brian?" Tanner said.

"Yeah, mate?"

"I'll kill all of you."

There was laughter from the men, followed by Brian's command. "Light 'em up!"

Five guns blasted away. Glass shattered, metal ruptured, and ricocheting rounds buried themselves in seats and the corpse of the pilot, Yaromir. Other bullets chewed at the ice and sent splinters of it scattering in all directions before the gunfire ceased. If not for the bulk of the engine protecting Tanner and Sara, the barrage would have been lethal.

Sara wanted to scream, but she kept it in. Still, she was trembling. Tanner felt her shivering as he held her, and knew it was caused by more than the frigid air that surrounded them.

Sara gazed about, as she looked for a way to escape. There was a rise of stone behind them, while trees were visible in the other directions, visible, but too far away to reach. If she and Tanner made a run for it, they would be cut to pieces by Brian and his friends.

And while they were both armed, they had to expose themselves to fire their weapons, which left them vulnerable. Then, there was the cold, which was another factor, and nothing prevented the helicopter pilot from going off to get more men, or perhaps joining the fight.

As tears filled her eyes, Sara looked at Tanner. "We're going to die."

He kissed her. "I won't let them hurt you."

Sara stared at him, incredulous that he could be so calm. Then, the fear left her, and she nodded once.

"I'm sorry. I forgot who I was with."

"I will kill them."

"Yes, although, I'll be damned if I know how you'll do it."

Tanner's eyes narrowed as he looked in Brian's direction. "It will be done with great pleasure."

2

POLINA

In the city of Novosibirsk, Pavel Krasotkin approached the chauffeur of a limousine with a purposeful stride. Like the chauffeur, Pavel was wearing a dark suit under a black wool coat, but also had on a fake beard that was made to look like that of the chauffeur, a man named Stas. Above the beard was a pair of dark sunglasses, even though the day was overcast with ominous clouds that warned of an approaching storm.

Stas carried a gun and was a karate and judo expert. He had finished a late lunch and was on his way to pick up his charge at the private school she attended. Although Stas was a limo driver, he was also a bodyguard. He had been trained in self-defense and held a black belt, while having also attained the fourth Dan level, which is called Yon Dan.

None of that training helped him in the least when Pavel Krasotkin attacked him. Pavel was an expert in a martial art called Combat Sambo, which was an amalgam of different disciplines. He was also lightning fast, dexterous, and strong.

Pavel took Stas down with a leg sweep that was too quick for the eye to follow. After slamming a gloved fist into the man's throat, Pavel smashed Stas' head against the ground.

Stas, who was balding, but powerfully built, struggled to stay conscious while reaching for his gun. Before he could clear the weapon from its holster, Pavel ended the battle by breaking the man's neck. He gave Stas' head a vicious twist with one arm while immobilizing his neck with the other.

Several patrons of the restaurant were in the parking lot, having just finished their meal. They gawked at Pavel as he calmly picked up the chauffeur's cap, but then ran back inside the restaurant when Pavel claimed Stas' gun.

The keys to the limo were in Stas' right front pocket. Pavel removed them as the man took his last gasping breath.

Two minutes later, Pavel was driving up to an unmanned gate at the rear of a private school. The limo was equipped with a sophisticated barcode that was read by a scanner, and a pair of wrought iron gates parted and let Pavel onto the property.

He spotted the girl easily, although the young teen was dressed the same as those around her. All of them were wearing the uniform of the Russian Girl Scout, dark blue slacks with a blouse of a lighter blue. They also wore ties that bore red, white, and blue stripes. The ties were held together by a brass clasp, which had the Girl Scouts' insignia stamped upon it.

The girl, Polina, also had many patches sewn onto her blouse, which were signs of merit and honor, and she was easily the most beautiful of the girls. Polina's blonde hair glistened in the sun while her pigtails made her look adorable.

Pavel sighed, he was not happy about having to abduct the child and would find the necessary act of killing her to be most distasteful. Nevertheless, he would commit both heinous crimes, because it served a greater purpose.

A teacher broke up the gathering by pointing to her watch and reminding the girls that they had a Girl Scout meeting to attend. Each of the girls went to their respective rides, most of which were other limousines.

Pavel had been planning Polina's abduction for weeks and was aware of her habits. So, he was not surprised when Polina approached with her head down as she looked at her phone. She was also carrying her jacket under her arm, knowing that the interior of the limo would be warm. Pavel, at her age, had rarely been warm with anything other than the heat of an open flame. He had also never ridden in any vehicle made after his birth, much less a new, chauffeur driven limousine.

As was another of her habits, before getting inside the limo, Polina looked up with a bright smile at her driver.

"Hi, Stas." The smile disappeared, to be replaced by a look of confusion that shown in her large green eyes. "You're not Stas."

Pavel jabbed her in the arm with the hypodermic needle he held. Polina's knees grew weak as her mouth went slack. He tumbled her into the rear of the limo, looked around, and saw that no one was paying him any attention.

The teacher who had reminded the girls of their meeting had dropped a folder, and papers were floating everywhere in the day's strong breeze. If any of those papers belonged to Polina, the teacher could let the breeze take them. Young Polina would never return to school.

The beautiful girl was out cold, and the drug would see that she stayed that way for some time. Pavel maneuvered the long vehicle into line behind others of its kind, many of which ferried about the future leaders of Russia. But not Polina, no, not Polina, for her short life would end in a matter of days, and in a place where she would likely never be found.

Pavel was taking her to a remote section of wilderness southeast of Barnaul. Unfortunately for Pavel, that area was not as sparsely populated as it usually was. He would soon cross paths with a man who was even deadlier than himself, an assassin named Tanner.

3
NO WORRIES, MATE

"Tannnnerrrr, come out, come out, wherever you are. Oh, wait, you're right over there, cowering behind that airplane engine like a regular pussy."

Brian chuckled at his own words, as his mates laughed along.

"What an asshole," Sara said, but Tanner was glad the man liked to talk. It gave him the time he needed to prepare.

"Me and the boys here all heard what a rip snorter of a hard ass you are. Some bullshit about how you killed a Mexican cartel leader. And oh yeah, now there's a rumor floating around that you whacked that arsehole Maurice Scallato. Bullshit I say, we got you easy. What did you do, Tanner, hire a PR firm to make that shit up? Now listen, mate, send out the woman. There's no reason she should die too… at least, not right away."

Sara spoke low enough so that only Tanner could hear her. "Matthews wants me alive so he can torture me. I had him beaten so he would give up the money he'd stolen from Conrad Burke."

Tanner slung an M16 across his back. It was loaded with a High-Capacity magazine that held 60 rounds. He then caressed Sara's cheek as he spoke to her and noted that her skin was as cold as the ice they were squatting on.

"Talk to this idiot while I get in position."

Sara looked him over. "I'm worried about you."

"I'll be fine. Besides, it's the only way we'll get out of this."

"Hey Tanner! Smith described that sheila of yours. I've got to say, she sounds hot, yes sir, I crack a fat just thinking about her."

"Brian," Sara said.

"The sheila speaks! What is it, luv?"

"The man who hired you, do you know his real name?"

"He said it was Smith and that's good enough for me. Now luv, are you ready to come on out from behind there? We'll warm you up, oh yes we will."

"If you touch me, I'll kill you."

"Ha, Smith said you were a tough bitch. He also wants to torture you. Me and me mates having a go at you might qualify as torture. There have been times when we've left a woman worse for wear."

"You're a pig, Brian."

The huge Aussie shivered and rolled his massive shoulders, as the cold began to penetrate his thick hide. "Tanner, come on now, let's finish this. And I've got to say, I was hoping you'd be more of a challenge."

Tanner's voice came from behind Brian. "No worries, mate."

The big man spun around just as Tanner opened fire. Brian caught the first rounds from the M16 across his stomach. Tanner moved the rifle right to left in an ascending path, which blew the head off the last of the men, while leaving the others with multiple torso wounds.

Firing the weapon accurately took more effort and control than normal, because Tanner was shivering.

He was almost naked but was wearing a pair of boxers along with his socks. He had entered the near-freezing water by the plane wreckage to swim under the lake ice and emerge out of the aperture the plane had made upon first impact.

While climbing out of the water, Tanner had been vulnerable. It had taken precious seconds for him to make it to his feet and shake the rifle free of water.

Sara had kept Brian occupied by talking to him and was overjoyed when she heard Tanner's voice. She had simply dipped her hand in the water when he told her his plan and felt her fingers go numb. As tough as he was, Sara had been afraid that Tanner would succumb to the cold before he could resurface.

She stepped from behind the plane's engine. The other four men were lying on the ice, while Brian was on his knees. When the Aussie attempted to reach for his rifle, he was struck from behind with shots fired by Sara, who then finished off one of the other men who was screaming in agony.

Meanwhile, Tanner had turned and let loose three rounds at the helicopter. His goal had been to scare the pilot into giving up. Instead, the pilot, who had been looking on aghast at the turn of events, became animated. The chopper rose into the sky and flew away.

Sara went to Tanner with his clothes under her arm, including fresh underwear. She also carried the bag that contained their weapons. After setting the clothes on top of the bag to keep them dry, she wiped away the water on Tanner's skin.

"Let me dry you off first with this T-shirt. Oh, how cold you must be. The water on your skin is turning to ice."

Tanner's teeth chattered as his body convulsed, then, he spoke with difficulty. "Help me… with the rifle first… it's stuck to my hands."

Sara winced as she held the M16 and watched Tanner rip his hands free of the cold metal. She had no doubt that he'd left some skin behind on the gun.

"Plane, Yaromir… he had a thermos of something."

"Yes! I remember, I'll get it," Sara said.

Sara returned to the plane and realized for the first time that she was limping. Adrenaline had anesthetized her from the pain of her knee injury, but it was making itself known. She moaned with sadness as she looked at Yaromir's ravaged body, while also removing the thermos from the floor of the plane. The blue plastic thermos was dented, but intact, and she could hear liquid sloshing around inside it.

Tanner was putting on his boots over fresh socks by the time she returned. Sara gave him some of what looked like soup from the lid of the thermos. As soon as the warm liquid entered him, the shivering ceased.

"Ah, that's good," Tanner said. "It's kharcho, it's a soup made with lamb and rice."

Sara took a sip, then made a face of surprise. "It's tangy, but the warmth feels lovely going down."

A soft moan came from their right. It was Brian, who still clung to life.

Tanner walked over, grabbed the man by his blond hair, then slid him across the ice, and toward the hole he had climbed out of minutes earlier.

"It's time for you to return down under," Tanner said.

Brian made a gurgling sound that might have been a

protest, but it had no sway with Tanner. He shoved the big man head first into the water.

Afterwards, they finished the soup and got busy gathering up supplies. This included taking a set of boots off one of the dead men and exchanging the frozen M16 for Brian's AK-47. After that, they sent Brian's fellow mercs into the water to join him.

The boots were for Sara, who put them on over three sets of thick socks, since the stylish shoes she had been wearing were no good for the rugged terrain they faced.

Their cell phones were useless, as there were no relay towers nearby. As they gazed around, they saw only nature looking back at them.

Tanner pointed a gloved hand northward. "We'll head back toward Barnaul. We should get a cell signal long before we reach it."

"How far do you think it is?"

"I'm not sure, but it's certainly not close. Damn me for not paying more attention."

"We'll be fine. The threat is over."

"No, this won't be over until Matthews or whoever hired Brian is dead. If it was Matthews, he must have spotted us in Barnaul and thought we were there looking for him. That assumption will cost him his life."

Tanner and Sara headed north across the frozen lake and toward a forest of pines. They were unaware that a snowstorm had shifted direction and was heading their way, and equally oblivious to the fact that Brian and his friends were only the beginning of the threats they would face.

4
WHAT DO YOU MEAN THEY'RE DEAD?

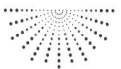

The helicopter pilot who had flown Brian and the other men to what would be their doom, relayed their fate to Dan Matthews, whom he knew by the name of Smith. They were standing inside a large airplane hangar on a private airfield, which the pilot owned, along with two partners.

The pilot was named Fedor. Fedor was a good-looking devil with a rakish smile. His sense of adventure had often gotten him into trouble, both in and out of bed. Fedor's current love interest was a sexy blonde named Liliya. Liliya had walked out on her husband to be with Fedor, who she found exciting.

Liliya's ex-husband was named Nikolai. Nikolai was Fedor's partner in the airfield, he was also a pilot and mechanic.

Liliya pointed at the bullet marks in the helicopter's windshield. "You were fired at?"

"After Tanner killed the Australians he turned his gun on me. I got the hell out of there. Smith, you might want to leave Barnaul and head somewhere else."

Dan Matthews looked disgusted by the turn of events. He had spent a good chunk of the remaining money he had hiring the Australian mercenaries. It was money he'd come by after breaking into the home of an old friend and robbing him. The friend had been a hoarder of gold coins, who foolishly kept them in velvet-lined drawers in his basement rec room.

Matthews had left the house while carrying away over twenty pounds of gold, just seconds before the police arrived. Most of that money went to purchasing a new identity and leaving America. Then, just when he felt safe, he spotted Sara Blake with Tanner as they came out of a hotel.

At first, Matthews didn't know who Tanner was. He had seen a sketch of the man, had talked to him on the phone, but had never met him in person. He asked a bartender in the hotel's lounge if he knew the man's name.

The bartender had a stocky build with a trim beard and ready smile. He told Matthews he wasn't allowed to discuss the hotel's guests with anyone. Matthews slid enough Russian rubles across the bar to loosen the man's tongue and the bartender leaned forward and whispered.

"He's checked in under the name Thomas Myers."

Matthews searched his memory for anyone he'd known with that name and came up blank. Perhaps Sara Blake wasn't after him but was simply in Russia as a tourist.

"Thanks. Is there anything else you can tell me about the man or the woman?"

The bartender grinned. "I can tell you I wish she were my woman."

Matthews had frowned at that. Sara Blake was beautiful, and he had fantasized about her himself on occasion, that is, before she had him beaten to a pulp. Since then, all he felt toward the woman was hatred.

Matthews turned away from the bar, but the bartender called him back.

"Mister."

"What?"

"The lady, she calls the man by another name."

"What, like a nickname?"

"I don't think so. It's a proper surname."

Matthews leaned over the bar again. "What is it?"

The bartender's grin was huge. "I'm sorry, but as I said before, I'm not allowed to—"

Matthews tossed more money at the man before he could finish his act.

"Tell me the other name before I lose my temper."

The bartender had scooped up the money and laughed. He was several inches taller than Matthews, had more muscle, and was years younger. "You couldn't beat me up on the best day of your life."

"No, but I can hire men to come here and break you into pieces. Do you understand me?"

The bartender's face lost its humorous expression and he spoke in a monotone. "Thomas Myers, the lady calls him by the name of Tanner."

"Tanner? Are you certain?"

"Yes."

The fact that Sara and Tanner were a couple hadn't surprised Matthews, since Sara Blake was the one who had recommended the Burke Corporation hire the hit man. How Blake and Tanner had tracked him down he couldn't imagine, and there was no way he could leave them alive. If Tanner was involved, it meant his life was at stake. As far as Matthews knew, it was kill or be killed.

Matthews feared Tanner more than he dreaded going back to prison. They wouldn't kill him in prison, but

Tanner would see him dead, unless Matthews acted to prevent that from happening.

Matthews left the hotel and took a cab toward the outskirts of town. There was a topless bar there where he knew he could find muscle to hire. That muscle had been Brian and his men.

"FEDOR," MATTHEWS SAID. "IF I GOT MORE MEN WOULD you be willing to fly them to where Tanner is?"

"First, you tell me the truth. Who is Tanner?"

"He's just a man I owe for causing me trouble."

"No, I heard the mercenaries talking in my helicopter. My English isn't great, but I know that they made Tanner sound like a big deal."

Matthews was about to lie, but then figured it was useless. "Tanner is a hit man, and apparently one hard bastard to kill. Although, many have tried."

A gleam entered Fedor's eyes. "So, killing this man would make one famous?"

"To those in the know, yes."

"Hmm, like the old-time gunslingers in your country. If you kill the fastest gun in the west, you become the fastest gun in the west."

"Something like that, yeah, so will you fly for me again?"

"Da, the same price as before. But, not in this chopper. I nearly froze to death with the door off, and I need to replace the windshield."

"Fly whatever you want. I'll be back soon. I think I know where I can get help."

Matthews left the hanger and Liliya wrapped her arms

around Fedor's neck. She had to reach up to do so, as she was nearly a foot shorter than her lover.

"I'll come too," Liliya said, "I'd love to get a look at this man, Tanner. He sounds like he's something else."

"What's this about Tanner?" said a voice from the doorway. The voice belonged to Nikolai, Liliya's ex-husband. Nikolai was a tall man with curly dark hair who wore a perpetual look of worry.

Nikolai saw Liliya more often than when they were married, because she spent most of her time hanging around Fedor. Liliya didn't know a thing about aviation, but she was a partner in the business, having been awarded half of Nikolai's fifty-percent interest during their divorce.

"That man, Tanner, he nearly shot Fedor out of the sky," Liliya said.

Nikolai's hands flew to his head as he gripped handfuls of hair. "Fedor, you idiot! I told you not to get involved with Smith and those damn Australians. What did they do, did they kill Tanner?"

"They weren't man enough, Nikolai," Liliya said. "But Fedor is, and he will hunt down Tanner and kill him."

Nikolai moved his head back and forth rapidly, as if to shake loose the words he'd just heard. "That's insane. Do you realize who Tanner is? They say he's the best killer in the world."

Liliya laughed, as she pantomimed holding an assault rifle. "He was better than the Australians, that's for sure. Fedor said he cut them all down with a machine gun while naked."

"Naked?" Nikolai said. "Whatever. Go after him, Fedor. Maybe Tanner will give you what you deserve."

Liliya hugged Fedor. "I'm going with him. I want to see him kill Tanner."

"No! Liliya, are you crazy? What if Tanner turns his gun on you?"

"Fedor will protect me."

"Fedor? Fedor is nothing but a punk."

Liliya laughed, then winked. "He's more of a man then you'll ever be, Nikolai, and in more ways than one."

Nikolai glared at Liliya, but there was no hate in his eyes. Even knowing that she had only married him because he had money hadn't killed his love for her. However, there was hate in Nikolai, and it was directed toward Fedor.

"Tell Liliya she can't go. It will be too dangerous for her."

"Liliya can do what she wants. I don't own her."

"It's not about owning her, you idiot; it's about keeping her safe."

Fedor smiled, but there was no humor in his eyes. "Do you remember the fight we had, Nikolai, or do I need to kick your ass again?"

Nikolai let out a huff, then spun on his heels and left the hanger.

"Fedor?"

"Yes, Liliya?"

"We need to find a new partner."

Fedor laughed. "I like the way you think."

The airfield bordered a piece of land where a strip club was located.

The dancing was a cover for the prostitution that went on behind the scenes. The club attracted the worst of the city's residents, while offering up some of its hottest women. Liliya had worked there for a time, until Nikolai fell in love with the stripper and married her.

The bar's founder was a man named Ivan Dumonovsky. Dumonovsky had been a shrewd man, who as a young boy, had lived through the hell that was the Siege of Leningrad. As a man, Ivan used his wits and fists to gain his wealth. Ivan passed away weeks earlier, and now his two sons owned the business.

They were Gleb and Aleksandr, the Dumonovsky brothers. Gleb and Aleksandr were not shrewd, couldn't fight worth a damn, and in a battle of wits, they'd be unarmed combatants. They were in their forties, and both were large, but doughy-looking, and their brown eyes were as dull as their brains. Both men wore beards. Aleksandr had a mustache, but Gleb had always been unable to grow more than peach fuzz on his upper lip.

Gleb's scraggly beard blended in with a pair of wide and bushy sideburns that were attached to a mop of unruly brown hair. The sideburns only brought attention to his ears, which were large. Gleb's ears stuck out like a pair of stubby wings on a fat bird. With his prominent eyebrow ridge, tiny nose, fleshy lips, and big teeth, he looked like a huge chimp.

Aleksandr, the younger of the two by one year, had fared better in the genetics lottery, but not by much, and it was easy to tell they were brothers.

Shortfalls aside, Gleb and Aleksandr did have money, along with the desire to be as respected and feared as their late father had been.

Matthews spoke to them in the strip club's large office. The two brothers sat behind an impressive wooden desk, while Matthews had settled into one of three comfortable wing chairs in front of it. The room's green carpeting was plush, the white walls looked recently painted, and the artwork adorning them was tasteful. However, the conversation took place with the office door sitting open.

Gleb had broken the door two nights ago while horsing around with one of the club's bouncers.

Matthews found the throb of the bar music distracting, but he tried to ignore it as he spoke with Gleb and Aleksandr.

"The men who kill Tanner will be living legends."

Gleb scratched his balls as he spoke. "This guy really killed those Australians, even that Brian, the one with the big mouth?"

"Yes, but see, Brian and his men must have softened Tanner up somewhat, and now he's out there in the middle of nowhere freezing to death. There will never be a better time to go after him."

Aleksandr swallowed a long drink of beer, belched, then had a question. "Why aren't you going after him, Smith?"

"Me? I'm not a tough guy like you two."

"Yeah, but the more guys we bring with us, the easier it will be to kill this guy, right?"

"Yes, and if you put the word out that there's a reputation to be gained by killing Tanner, I'm sure that many of those losers out there in the bar will go hunting for him."

"But we'll get the credit, right?" Gleb said.

"Of course," Matthews said. "So, what do you say?"

"What do we say about what?" Aleksandr said.

"About Tanner, will you pay for the gas and supplies we'll need to go after him?"

"Oh, yeah, Gleb and me got nothing else to do. Once we shoot this hit man, Tanner, everyone will know we're badasses, like our father was."

"Great, great, how many men do you think you can get?"

"A dozen easy, there's a huge biker gang out there. Those guys are always up for trouble."

There was a scuff of footsteps coming from the hallway behind Matthews, then a voice spoke in a resigned tone.

"Make it two dozen men. I'll be going after Tanner too."

Matthews turned in his seat and saw Nikolai standing just inside the doorway.

"What are you talking about, Nikolai? You suddenly have an interest in Tanner?"

"I have an interest in keeping my wife safe, and that idiot Fedor is taking her off on the hunt for this hit man. If I can kill Tanner first, Liliya will stay safe."

"She's your ex-wife. You're only trying to beat Fedor at something. But, whatever, I just want Tanner dead, you and Fedor can work out the details."

"No, I'm going with my own group."

Gleb laughed. The sound was reminiscent of a toilet flushing. "We'll have an army chasing after this guy, Tanner."

Matthews nodded, then wondered if an army would be enough.

5
WHY AREN'T YOU WEARING MASKS?

Walking along in the cold, Tanner and Sara tried to maintain a steady pace without perspiring under the many layers they wore. As cold as it was, sweating was a bad idea, as it could chill the skin and lower the body's core temperature.

They had gone through their luggage and found that many of their clothes were too wet to wear, as the luggage compartment had taken on water after the crash. They had managed to salvage some clothing, and it would have to do until they found shelter.

There were wolves nearby. They could be heard now and then as they howled to each other, and once, Tanner glimpsed a pack of them, but they were just silhouettes against the backdrop of the trees in the distance.

Walking was harder for Sara, whose knee was beginning to ache with each step. To keep her mind off it, she asked Tanner to tell her more about the hunting trip he'd gone on as a boy.

"What was that girl's name?"

"It was Genevieve."

"Did you ever talk to her, or chicken out?"

"I talked to her. My voice was shaky at first, but I spoke to her."

"What did you say?"

"I said my name is Cody Parker."

Genevieve smiled at Cody, then looked him up and down. "You're a little taller than me. How old are you?"

"I'm twelve."

"I thought you looked young, and you say your name is Cody?"

"That's right, and I heard you were named Genevieve."

"Yeah, I was named after Saint Genevieve, the patron saint of Paris. She protected Paris from Attila the Hun."

"How'd she do that?"

"She prayed."

Cody nodded, but was no longer listening. Genevieve was so beautiful that he found himself mesmerized by her. He snapped out of it when Genevieve waved her hand in front of his face.

"Hey, kid, are you all right?"

"I'm not a kid. I'm just young."

Genevieve laughed. "Okay, so, do you like to hunt?"

"Yeah, and I'm gonna get a buck too."

"A buck?"

"You know, a male deer."

"Oh, right. I've never hunted, but my mom has. She grew up doing it."

"Can you shoot?"

Genevieve made a sour face. "The rifle hurts my shoulder."

The guide of the hunt gathered all the participants together and told them that they would have a chance to sight-in their rifles if they wanted to. There were several targets lined up in an area before a hill. As always, the sighting-in of rifle scopes turned into a shooting contest. To everyone's surprise but his grandfather, Cody Parker was the best shooter by far.

When Cody finished, he received many "Attaboy's" from the men, and to his delight, he had gained a female fan. Genevieve came over to him with a huge grin, then kissed him on the cheek.

"Wow! Cody, you're something else with that rifle."

Cody smiled back at Genevieve, neither of them noticed the man staring at them. Rather, he was staring at Genevieve, as he had been doing all morning from a spot in the woods. The man was stalking her, and when the time was right, he planned to make Genevieve his next victim.

"A RAPIST?" SARA SAID.

"And a murderer, he had killed in Colorado before coming to Texas. The girls there had been only eleven and thirteen."

"What happened to Genevieve?"

Tanner was about to answer Sara when something attracted his attention. He pointed east, where the land sat higher along a ridge.

"Look! Do you see that, that flash of sunlight?"

Sara covered her eyes with her hand, then broke into a smile.

"That looked like a small plane landing."

"It was. There must be an airfield over there."

"How far away is that?"

"Three miles, maybe a little less."

"I say we check it out."

"Yeah, but stay alert when we get close. Anyone living out here probably doesn't want visitors, and we have no idea what they might be up to."

"You mean drug smuggling?"

"Maybe, but there's some reason they're out here in the middle of nowhere."

THAT REASON INVOLVED THE KIDNAPPING OF A FOURTEEN-year-old girl named Polina. The abductor of the girl, Pavel, flew her to a secluded location where he believed no one would be searching for her. Pavel landed his small plane on a large frozen lake that was some distance from the lake where Tanner and Sara had crashed. This lake was surrounded by sloping land on all sides, as it was located on the ridge.

There were people living in the area, but they numbered less than a hundred and made their homes farther back in the woods.

The lake tended to overflow in springtime, and in the winter, the icy wind coming off the frozen lake was brutal. Because of this, people in the area built their homes along the streams that weaved through the woods, where the trees acted as a natural windbreak.

As Pavel carried Polina from the plane, the teen stirred awake.

"What's going on?"

"You've been kidnapped," Pavel said. He was clean-shaven, as he had discarded the phony beard he'd been wearing.

Polina seemed to have no reaction to the news of her kidnapping. Pavel looked down at her, wondering if she had drifted back to sleep. When Polina's fist connected with his nose, he let out a grunt of annoyance and dropped her onto the ground.

Polina attempted to stand, but the drug Pavel injected her with earlier was still having an influence on her. She found it difficult to maintain her balance. Polina staggered, dropped to one knee, staggered again, then fell on her stomach. When she glanced up, she saw two men approaching with guns holstered on their hips. The men were wearing fur hats with earflaps.

When they spoke to Pavel, they did so in Turkish. Polina didn't speak Turkish, but she had heard the language spoken between students and one of the teachers at her school. She recognized the language when she heard it.

One of the Turks, the shorter of the two, reared back his boot as if he were going to kick Polina in the side. A sharp rebuke from Pavel froze the man. Afterward, Pavel helped Polina to stand.

When Polina looked at Pavel, she frowned. His nose had not bled. Her punch seemed to have had no effect on the man.

"You're all in a lot of trouble," Polina said in Russian.

Pavel smiled. "Because of who your grandmother is?"

"That's right. She's important, and you'll go to prison for this."

"We will never be caught. If you're a smart little girl, you will be quiet and give us no trouble."

"I'm smart enough to know that people will be looking for me. And they'll find me too."

Pavel extended an arm and gestured about at their

surroundings. "Look about, Polina. You are no longer in the city and there is no one around for many miles."

Polina gazed left, then right. Other than a large tent with a fire burning near it, she saw nothing but the lake, woodland, and the small airplane she'd been transported in. The realization that she may never be rescued sent a chill of terror through her, but then a question popped into her head.

"How did you get the limo away from Stas?"

"Your chauffeur is dead. I broke the man's neck to prove we were serious."

Tears sprang from Polina's eyes. "You murdered Stas? You bastard!"

Polina tried to strike Pavel again, but this time the man's hands were free. He blocked her attempt with ease, then backhanded her on the chin. Polina's blonde pigtails went flying in all directions as her head was rocked backwards.

She would have fallen again, as the impact of Pavel's hand stunned her, and made her taste blood. But Pavel lifted her up once more, this time, to toss her over his shoulders in the position called a fireman's carry. Polina fought to stay awake as she watched the ground flow by while Pavel marched into the woods.

After Pavel stopped walking, Polina felt an odd sensation and clutched onto Pavel. She was falling. No, not falling, but going down a ladder while lying over Pavel's shoulders. As her head cleared, she felt rope being fastened to her right wrist, then saw a knot being tied that only a knife could free her from. She was in a large deep pit that had a rotted wood floor and dirt walls.

Pavel lowered her onto an old mattress, and there was a small stack of thick wool blankets, some bottled water, a battery-powered lantern, toilet paper, and, incongruously, a toilet.

Pavel saw the puzzled look on Polina's face and almost smiled. He pointed at the toilet, which was in a corner, at the farthest range of the rope.

"There's no plumbing attached, of course, but we dug a deep hole beneath it. This was once a root cellar or a basement. Someone long ago made the foolish decision to build near the lake. The house is gone, likely washed away over the years, but this pit remains and will be your new home."

Polina watched Pavel ascend the rope ladder and wondered if the man was a gymnast. She doubted there were chimpanzees that could climb the ladder with such speed and grace of movement.

Pavel looked down at her and offered advice. "Try to remain calm. If you behave, no one will hurt you."

"When will you send me back to my family?"

"As soon as your grandmother follows our orders."

"My grandmother will pay you."

"We don't want her money. We want her obedience."

"Please let me out of here."

"Goodbye, Polina."

"Wait!"

"What is it?"

Polina hesitated before speaking, as she feared Pavel's response to her next query.

"Why aren't you wearing masks?"

Pavel sighed. "You're a smart girl. I think you already know the answer to that question."

There was the creak of hinges, then a wooden cover fell with a loud thump, covering the opening. That was followed by the sound of something locking the lid in place.

If not for the lantern, Polina would have been in pitch blackness. Out of habit, she reached for her cell phone, but it was gone. The pit stank of damp earth. Despite its greater size and depth, it reminded Polina of a grave.

Polina tried to be brave, but the tears came anyway. She hugged herself, and as she did so, she felt the patches on her uniform blouse, patches she had earned as a Girl Scout.

In her mind, Polina went over the ten Girl Scout laws.

A Girl Scout is true to her word.

A Girl Scout finishes what she starts.

A Girl Scout strives to be useful and to help others.

A Girl Scout is friendly, cordial, and polite.

All Girl Scouts are sisters.

A Girl Scout is a friend of nature.

A Girl Scout is devoted to her parents, is disciplined, and obeys her leader.

A Girl Scout is thrifty and respects the property of others.

A Girl Scout is clean and noble in her thoughts and actions.

When she reached the last one, Polina dried her eyes and repeated the tenth law out loud.

"A Girl Scout never loses heart."

Someone would find her. Polina was certain of it. Maybe a policeman, a soldier, or one of the government agents that worked with her grandmother. She would be found and set free.

After all, wasn't the world full of heroes?

6

HALF A BRAIN BETWEEN THEM

Tanner climbed up a tree to get a better look at the area where the plane was. He'd seen Pavel backhand Polina. However, he had been too far away to make out any details of the pair, or of the two Turks with them.

"They've got a girl or a small woman over there and one of them took her down into a hole."

"A hole?"

"Yeah, some sort of pit, maybe even a tunnel. It's hard to see from here."

"Do you think it has anything to do with Matthews?"

Tanner dropped to the ground beside Sara, his landing cushioned by the snow.

"No, but they're up to something. The good news is the plane. It's parked on another frozen lake. We can force them to fly us out of here."

"How many men did you see?"

"Only three, but there could be more inside the tent they have."

They began walking again, and Sara's limp was more noticeable.

"How bad is your knee?" Tanner asked.

"It hurts, but I can push on until we reach that plane."

"Fine, but don't push too hard. You may be more injured than you know. Cold weather like this is a natural anesthetic."

"Let's just get to that plane," Sara said.

Pavel had informed his companions that there was a winter storm heading into the area, but that it wouldn't begin in earnest until after midnight.

"Will you be able to fly in such weather," asked the taller of the two men.

"I'll likely be grounded, but I have the other snowmobile. I'll return one way or another. Just stay inside the tent, and you'll be warm enough."

The shorter of the Turks pointed at the fire, where two blocks of stone were being heated by the flame. The blocks looked like granite, but were soapstone, which held heat well and for many hours.

"Those stones will really work?"

"Yes, but don't let them stay in the flames too long."

The taller Turk gazed in the direction of the pit. "She may freeze down there."

"Not overnight, and she has the blankets. After we film her crying and begging tomorrow, it won't matter what happens to her."

"I don't like hurting children, but we do what is necessary," said the tall man.

"Yes, my brother, and that is why we'll triumph and change the course of history. We are willing to do what is necessary."

Pavel shook hands with the men, glanced in the

direction of the pit, which was disguised to blend in with the ground, then he turned and headed toward the plane.

"What plane?" Gleb asked. He and his brother Aleksandr were in the hanger with Fedor and Liliya.

"That one, the one with the big red cross on it," Fedor said, while pointing to his left. "It was an old rescue plane Nikolai bought for spare parts, but I've been getting it into shape and she'll fly just fine."

"So what?" Gleb asked.

Fedor laughed. "Don't you see? When Tanner looks up and sees this plane, he'll come running while thinking he's saved. His guard will be down."

"Why?" Aleksandr said.

Liliya was seated by a soft drink machine and doing her nails. Fedor looked over at Liliya and saw her roll her eyes. She had warned Fedor that the brothers had half a brain between them, and that he'd have to speak to them like he was talking to children, and dim-witted children at that.

"That big red cross, it's the international symbol of humanitarian aid, like medical doctors and rescue workers. Tanner will think we're there to rescue him, get it?"

"Oh," Gleb said. "But we'll really be there to kill him, right?"

"Riiiight," Fedor said, as he wondered who tied Gleb's shoes every morning.

Aleksandr called to Liliya. "You should come back and dance sometime. We miss you."

"I bet it's not my dancing you miss."

Gleb stared at her. "I liked seeing you naked."

Liliya smiled. "All men do, but I'm a businesswoman now, and only Fedor gets to see me naked."

"That's not fair," Aleksandr said. "But the new girls are hot too."

Fedor stepped in front of the brothers and blocked their view of Liliya. "Get your men ready. We'll be leaving soon."

"How many men can you fit in that thing?" Gleb asked.

"You and your brother bring ten men along."

Gleb giggled. "We got a surprise for Tanner, hand grenades, three of them, our father kept them in the safe."

Fedor smiled. "Hand grenades. That should do the trick."

"What trick?" Aleksandr asked.

Fedor held up his hands and wiggled his fingers. "Remember, bring back this many men, and no more than that. We'll leave as soon as I fuel up the plane."

Gleb peeked around Fedor to smile at Liliya. He looked like a happy gibbon. "See you later, Liliya."

"Bye-bye, Gleb."

The two brothers left and Fedor shook his head in wonder. "They are dolts."

"Yeah, but they're rich dolts, so stay friendly with them."

"That Gleb leers at you. Just how friendly were you with him when you worked at their club?"

"I let him touch me sometimes, but when I worked there, it was his father I had to keep happy. I'm so glad that old bastard is dead."

"Is that why you married Nikolai, to get away from the old man?"

"Yeah, and was Nikolai ever boring. But then I met you, and you're never boring."

Fedor took Liliya by the arm and pulled her into the office. The small room contained two scarred wooden desks, along with chairs made of knotty pine. There were also a pair of metal filing cabinets and an old black leather sofa with a jagged tear in one arm. A corner bookcase held aviation repair manuals, several old instruments, and an empty beer can that Fedor had placed on a shelf weeks ago.

In the center of the room was a round braided rug that was multi-hued but filthy, since it had never been vacuumed. Above the rug was a ceiling fan that hadn't worked in years.

After he shut and locked the office door, Fedor sat on the sofa and smiled up at Liliya.

"Do what you do best."

Liliya checked to make sure her nail polish had dried, then, she lowered herself to the floor between Fedor's knees.

Tanner and Sara were still half a mile away when they heard the plane's engine. Given the cold temperature, Pavel had never shut it off. However, when the pitch changed, Tanner understood that they had arrived too late. That became evident as the airplane moved off across the lake's surface, then lifted into the air.

Sara swore in frustration. "Damn it. I hope the pilot comes back."

"He might," Tanner said. "The other two men are still there by the fire, but I want to get a look inside that pit first. Whoever is in there can give us some answers."

After a quick search of the area south of the tent, Tanner located the covered pit. The men had done an excellent job of camouflaging the pit's entrance. If he had not known the general area where it was located, Tanner doubted he would have stumbled upon it. As for the rope ladder, it was hanging from a tree limb and made to look like vines. The cover over the pit was locked down by a tree branch passed through two loops of rope. A crude lock, but effective.

Tanner handed Sara the AK-47 while he gripped the edge of the square covering with both hands and lifted it up. To Tanner's surprise, the lid had hydraulic support arms which helped to raise the weight and keep it from falling backwards.

With the lid open, Tanner stared down inside the pit and saw a pair of large green eyes looking up at him. It was a girl all right, a pretty thing with blonde pigtails.

Along with the fear in her eyes, Tanner saw a look of hope.

7

TO THE RESCUE

Polina stood up from the mattress when she heard the lid of the pit moving. She then squinted as the dull light of a cloudy sky poured in from above.

There was a man up there, a handsome man with unusual eyes. Polina blinked at the man, but said nothing, while thinking he might be another of the men who had imprisoned her. When he disappeared, she nearly cried out for him to come back, but then he was there again and tossing down the rope ladder.

"Can you climb?" he asked in Russian.

"Maybe, but I'm dizzy. That other man gave me something, a drug I think."

The man spoke English to someone that Polina couldn't see, then came down inside the pit in a flash. His speed reminded her of the man who had abducted her. She wondered what made them both so graceful.

"Are you one of them?" Polina asked.

Tanner cut the rope on her wrist. It had been tight, as Polina had been struggling to free herself.

"We're here to get you out. I'm Tanner, and there's a woman up top named Sara."

Polina smiled. "My grandmother sent you."

"No. Our plane crashed miles from here and we saw your plane land."

"Oh, but you will help me?"

"We need to get out of this pit before one of the men show up. Put your arms around my neck and lock your legs around my waist."

Polina did as she was told, then marveled at how fast they went up. He was not a huge man like her late chauffeur, Stas, but this man Tanner was strong. It was as if her weight made no difference to him at all.

Once they were up top, Polina saw the woman the man had spoken of. She was beautiful. When the woman smiled, followed by a sound of sympathy concerning her bruised chin, Polina knew they wouldn't hurt her.

"What's your name?" the man asked.

"I am Polina Nabokov and those men kidnapped me from Novosibirsk."

"You're safe now, and like I said before, I'm Tanner and this is Sara. We're Americans. Do you speak English?"

"I do," Polina said in Russian, then she giggled and spoke English. "I speak English well, thank you."

"Stay here with Sara, Polina. I'll go deal with those men and see if we can bring that pilot back here."

"Tanner, that pilot, he is a dangerous man."

"I understand, but I can handle myself. Don't worry, kid. Sara and I will make sure you get back home."

Polina grinned and hugged Tanner while laying her head on his chest. After releasing him, she stood on her tiptoes and kissed him on the lips.

"My hero."

Sara laughed, while Tanner raised an eyebrow and asked a question.

"What did you say your last name was, Nabokov?"

Polina nodded.

"Like the writer?" Sara asked.

"What writer?" Polina said.

"Never mind," Tanner said. "And here, take my jacket, Polina. You'll freeze to death wearing only that uniform."

Polina put on the jacket, then blushed as she thanked Tanner.

"Be careful," Sara said.

"Careful, but quick, I'll be right back."

Tanner moved off through the trees with the rifle leading the way. When he was out of sight, Polina spoke to Sara.

"He is very cute."

"Yes, and he's my boyfriend."

"What is he, a soldier?"

"Tanner, well… he's self-employed."

Polina snuggled inside the warmth of Tanner's jacket and sighed. "My hero."

The two Turks were crouched by the fire and heating tea in a pan.

Tanner came across a large snowmobile at the rear of the tent. If it was in working condition, he could ride out of the area with Sara and Polina, since there was snow on the ground.

Tanner spoke many languages, but Turkish wasn't one of them, so he had no idea what the men were saying. They, however, had no trouble understanding his meaning, as Tanner approached them with the AK-47 held at the ready.

The men appeared to be startled as they stood and looked around to see if Tanner were alone. The taller of the Turks right hand twitched, but he stopped himself from reaching for his gun, a Makarov pistol with a rubber grip. His shorter companion didn't display the same good sense. As his hand closed around his weapon, Tanner shot him twice in the chest.

The tall Turk put his hands up and pleaded with Tanner in Russian. "Don't shoot me!"

"Toss your gun over here… slowly."

The Turk complied, as his partner lay by the fire and moaned.

"The pilot that flew off, what's his name?"

The tall Turk glared at Tanner. "I will tell you nothing."

Tanner fired two more bullets into the man he'd shot. The moaning stopped.

A string of what Tanner assumed were Turkish curses issued forth from the other man, and he gazed at Tanner with a look of defiance.

"Kill me too, but I will not talk."

Tanner cocked his head. There was something more going on here than a simple kidnapping.

"How much was the ransom for the girl?"

The man spat on the ground in indignation. When he spoke, his voice was filled with a tone of righteous anger. "Money? This was not about money. Not everything is about money. Some of us have principles and vision."

"And some of us kidnap little girls and throw them down inside pits, but why that little girl?"

"I'll only say this. It concerns politics."

Tanner sighed. "Oh, so you're another damned terrorist."

"And what are you, you who kill with such ease?"

"I'm not a man that hurts children."

"The sacrifice of that child will save the lives of many children. Her grandmother is a member of the Russian Federation Council. If she follows our orders, the world will be a better place."

"So you say, but that won't happen. Polina is going back to her family and you'll have no leverage over her grandmother."

The Turk swiveled his head. "How did you get here? It certainly wasn't by plane or snowmobile. We would have heard it."

"The only plane I care about is yours. When is it coming back?"

"It will not return for many days. There is a snowstorm on the way."

Tanner shook his head once. "He'll be back. Polina's grandmother will want Proof of Life. My guess is he'll return here tomorrow with a current newspaper and film her holding it. That will reassure the family and prove that she's still living."

The Turk looked sullen, and Tanner knew he had guessed right.

"What's your name?" Tanner said.

The Turk stood straight and proud. "I am Ahmet Demirr. I am not a terrorist, but a freedom fighter."

"More like a martyr," Tanner said, then he blasted a bullet through Ahmet's heart.

Nikolai was about to board an ancient Cessna that he planned to jam ten men aboard, although the plane was rated to hold only seven. To beat Fedor to the crash site where the Australians died, Nikolai hoped to leave first, since he had an idea of where to look after having spoken to Matthews.

Except for his cousin, an ex-soldier named Volya, the men Nikolai was ferrying to the site were a bunch of lowlifes, but they were lowlifes with weapons. Hard to kill or not, once Tanner faced-off against ten guns, plus the weapons of Fedor's men, the hit man would die.

Nikolai took a deep breath, then released it slowly, as he readied himself for what lay ahead. The thought of killing depressed him. He had killed before, while in the army and fighting in The Second Chechen War. Although, he had practically been a boy then and had a lust for adventure.

The reality of war curbed his appetite for violence, but there was nothing he wouldn't do if it meant he might win back Liliya's heart. He had to reach Tanner first, had to be the man who killed him. Then, he would be someone exciting. The man who killed Tanner would be respected, perhaps feared, and Liliya couldn't possibly think him boring then.

Nikolai checked his weapon as he prepared to climb into the cockpit. The weapon was a Serbu Super Shorty. The small shotgun held three rounds. If he couldn't kill Tanner with that, the man was indestructible.

"Nikolai?"

It was Liliya. She was dressed in boots and wearing Fedor's flight jacket. On her petite frame, the jacket hung like a coat.

"Hello Liliya. Please tell me that you've decided to stay here."

Liliya came close to him, and as always, Nikolai was struck by how beautiful she was.

"It's you I'm worried about, Nikolai. Why are you going after Tanner?"

Nikolai shrugged. "To keep you safe. If I kill the man, then he'll have no chance to harm you."

"Why would Tanner want to kill me?"

"I mean accidentally, or maybe even on purpose. Who knows how a man like that thinks. He makes his living by dealing death."

"You're really worried about me?"

"Of course I am. You know that I love you."

Liliya paced for a few moments, paused, looked at Nikolai, then paced again. Nikolai watched her, while wondering what was going through her mind. After more pacing and silent looks, Liliya walked over and took Nikolai by the hand.

"Come with me to the office."

"Why?"

"I want to be alone with you, that's why."

A silly grin spread across Nikolai's face. Once they were in the office, Liliya shut the door and locked it. She sat on the sofa and gazed up at him.

"Get naked, Nikolai, then show me how much you love me."

Nikolai shed his thermal coveralls and the clothes beneath them in record time. As he did so, Liliya had unzipped her jacket. She was slowly, teasingly raising the hem of the thick sweater beneath it, revealing her flat stomach and the lower portion of her bra.

After Nikolai removed his socks, Liliya scooped up Nikolai's clothes, deftly unlocked the door, and ran from the office. She was giggling like a child.

"Liliya?"

"You're a fool, Nikolai. I was just buying time for Fedor to get ready. Hear that roar? That's the sound of Fedor's plane."

"Damn it, Liliya! Give me my clothes back."

"I'll leave them on the tarmac. The wind shouldn't scatter them too much. Bye-bye, Nikolai... lover boy."

Liliya's laughter cut as deep as her callousness, and it made Nikolai furious. Nikolai marched outside naked and gathered up his clothes. That is, most of his clothes. The wind had taken one of his socks to places unknown.

After boarding his plane and starting the engine, he was subjected to being the brunt of his passengers' jokes. With his engine still warming, Nikolai watched Fedor take off.

Any reticence he had over killing was gone. He would kill Tanner, oh yes, he damn sure would. And, if the son of a bitch so much as looked at him sideways, he would put down Fedor as well.

A minute after Fedor's plane disappeared into the gray clouds overhead, Nikolai was racing down the runway. He was mad enough to kill and had every intention of doing so.

8
LOLITA

After dealing with the two Turks, Tanner dragged their bodies over to the edge of the lake.

The men had a hatchet, and Tanner used it to chop a hole in the ice. To his surprise, the ice wasn't as thick as the ice had been at the lake where he'd taken his swim. He realized why as he recalled the sheer wall of rock that had bordered one side of the first lake. That barrier kept the lake in shadow hours longer than the lake he was currently at, still, the ice was many inches thick and could hold an aircraft or a hoard of ice-skaters.

Before disposing of the bodies, Tanner had searched both men and found the keys to the snowmobile, a compass, and spare ammo for their Makarov pistols. One of the guns was a lost cause, since it had been neglected for years and was filthy with grime. Tanner tossed it into the lake along with its owner.

The other gun, the one that had belonged to the proud and dedicated Ahmet Demirr, was in fine condition. Tanner decided to wear it on his hip.

Tanner discovered treasure inside the tent. There was

bottled water and juice, a few sticks of beef jerky, Russian MRE's, and the blocks of soapstone that Pavel had heated. The hunks of stone warmed the tent well. Tanner decided that they would pack one away for their trip north, just in case the snowmobile died and placed them back on foot. There was also extra clothing in the tent. Several sweatshirts and sweatpants, and a black hoodie that looked worn, but warm.

The trip would be considerably shorter now that they had the snowmobile. However, before taking the time to investigate the vehicle, Tanner went back to the pit to get Sara and Polina.

THE SOUND OF GUNSHOTS HAD WORRIED POLINA, BUT SARA assured her that Tanner would be all right and return to them before too long.

"But it was two against one. What if they hurt him?"

"Tanner has faced tougher odds and come out on top," Sara said with a smile.

Still, Polina was worried. Therefore, when she saw Tanner approaching and looking none the worse for wear, she was so full of joy that she rushed to meet him and hug him.

"It's all good, kid," Tanner said. "I even found food, of a sort."

"Of a sort?" Sara said. "What's that mean?"

"They're Russian MRE's, Meals Ready to Eat. If they're anything like the American version, they won't be too bad. Anyway, we need all the food we can get to fight the cold."

Minutes later, they were huddled around the fire and eating from the MRE's. Along with the food, which included salt, pepper, and sugar packets, the MRE's also had packs of wet napkins, matches, anti-bacterial tablets, dried fuel tablets to start fires, and three spoons.

They all ate the crackers with their meal, which consisted of meat loaf, a potato dish of some sort, and grits. There was also tea, and Polina grinned when Tanner handed her the lone fruit stick for dessert.

All in all, the meal wasn't bad, and the dried fuel tablets, along with the matches, were priceless out in the wilderness.

Polina sat as close to Tanner as she could get, and once she had eaten, she leaned her head against his shoulder. The beautiful teen hung on his every word and smiled at him shyly whenever he looked her way.

"I'm sleepy," Polina said. "Maybe the drug that man gave me is still working."

"Maybe," Sara said. "But you have had a lot of excitement for one day."

"Tanner, what did you do with the other two men that were here?" Polina asked.

"They're dead, Polina. They'll never hurt you again."

Polina appeared surprised by Tanner's answer, but also pleased. The Turks had seemed heartless and were willing to use her to get what they wanted. If their actions resulted in their deaths, then so be it.

"That other man, the pilot, he said he killed my chauffeur, Stas. Stas was my friend and I loved him."

"I'm sorry you lost a friend," Tanner said, and as he spoke, he stood slowly, so Polina wouldn't fall over.

"Are you going to check out that snowmobile?" Sara asked.

"Yeah, and if it works, we should reach cell tower range in less than an hour."

Sara checked the sky, which had darkened due to thickening clouds.

"I would not want to be out here during a storm, and it will be dark soon too."

THE SNOWMOBILE WAS COVERED IN SEVERAL INCHES OF snow that must have fallen since its last use. Tanner brushed the snow off, checked beneath the hood, and found that the engine looked fine. After closing the hood, he checked the gas lever and felt that it was frozen into position. It came free with the application of a little pressure and would work well if the engine ran.

Before starting the engine, Tanner opened the vehicle's choke half way by adjusting a lever, because it was so cold. The engine was slow to come to life, but it started, and after closing the choke, Tanner left the metal beast alone to warm itself up.

Polina had cheered and clapped when it started, and both Sara and Tanner had smiled at her youthful enthusiasm. While the engine warmed, Tanner and Sara packed supplies in the small space beneath the snowmobile's seat, and in a backpack they'd found inside the tent.

Before heading out, Tanner spoke to Polina. "We may run into more trouble. If that happens, I need to know that you'll do whatever Sara and I tell you to do, understand?"

Polina's big green eyes looked earnestly at Tanner. After kissing him on the cheek, she hugged him.

"I will do whatever you say. You are my hero."

Tanner looked over at Sara and saw that she was smiling. He eased Polina's arms from around him and stared at her.

"If you hear me shout, 'Get down,' that will be the cue for you to drop to the ground. And if I say, 'Run', then sprint for cover as fast as you can, okay?"

"Yes, I understand, and I am not a little girl, Tanner. I am nearly a woman."

"How old are you?" Tanner said.

"I am fourteen… and a half. In Russia, that means I'm almost a woman."

"That's good, Polina, it also means I won't have to worry about you. Remember, if I shout, 'Get down,' you get down fast."

After releasing a sigh, Polina smiled up at Tanner. "I would do anything you asked of me, anything."

Tanner cocked an eyebrow at those words, as Sara covered her mouth to keep from laughing.

As they prepared to leave, Sara donned the backpack, which was fine with Polina. It gave her an excuse to sit behind Tanner on the snowmobile, while Sara sat behind her.

Polina wrapped her arms around Tanner's waist. Along with his jacket, Tanner had given her two sweatshirts and a pair of sweatpants to wear over her Girl Scout uniform. He'd also given Polina one of the fur hats salvaged from the dead Turks.

The hat was so big that it covered the teen's forehead, but it would keep her warm. Sara wore the other cap, and she had moaned with pleasure as the fur covered her freezing ears.

That left Tanner wearing layers of sweatshirts under a black hoodie, along with a wool knit cap that was dark green. Although he was wearing a hood, Tanner didn't want to wear it. The sides of the hood would block his peripheral vision, so he had pulled the rear of the knit cap down over his ears, to protect them from the wind as he rode.

After checking to make certain he could draw the gun on his hip easily, Tanner moved off across the lake, which had a thin layer of snow upon its frozen surface.

Sara spotted the plane first, and she tapped Tanner on the shoulder to get his attention. After slowing down, Tanner followed Sara's pointing finger and saw what looked like a rescue plane headed their way. The plane circled above them and appeared to be lining up to land on the lake.

Polina shouted, "We are rescued!" in Russian, as Tanner brought the snowmobile to a stop.

However, he kept the machine running. He considered using the flare gun he had salvaged from the plane he and Sara had crashed in, but figured it wasn't necessary as the pilot had obviously spotted them. The plane landed smoothly and used most of the lake up before it finally stopped. Then, another plane appeared, one without markings that designated it as a rescue plane. It was too big to be the plane flown by the man who had abducted Polina, so there was no concern that he might have returned. Tanner wondered if perhaps the planes had been aware of the kidnapper's destination and had been out searching for Polina.

They climbed off the snowmobile, walked a short distance, and stared at the planes. The aircraft were parked close together, and Tanner saw that they were both filled with men. That placed him on alert, although there was doubtless an explanation for the men being on the plane that didn't involve him.

When Liliya exited the rescue plane and smiled at him, Tanner felt better about things, but that ended as a man of average height left the plane with the rest of the men, all of whom held guns.

"The shortest of the men. That's Dan Matthews," Sara said.

"Polina, get behind me," Tanner said.

The teen obeyed, and as she took in all the guns and the hard looks of the men, whispered words escaped her. "I'm scared, Tanner."

"I won't let them hurt you," Tanner said.

Then, the men on the other plane came out onto the ice as if they'd been disgorged like something that had a bad taste.

Altogether, Tanner was looking at twenty-four armed men. One of them, a grinning hulking baboon of a man held a hand grenade. That was Gleb, while the woman, Liliya, appeared to be unarmed, but was looking him over as if he were a delicacy she would love to taste.

Tanner had the AK-47 up and ready to use. Beside him, Sara pointed her gun at Matthews. Less than a hundred feet separated the two groups.

There was some talk between the men in the separate groups, a raised voice, and afterwards, two smaller groups approached. They stopped walking when they were still several yards away.

One group comprised, Matthews, Gleb, Aleksandr, Fedor, and Liliya, while Nikolai approached with his cousin, Volya, who was a large red-headed man with a full beard. Joining Nikolai and Volya were two biker types. The shorter of the two bikers was trying to get a better look at young Polina, while ignoring Sara. Tanner made a mental note to put the man down the first chance he got.

Matthews spoke, and did so in English, while looking back and forth at Tanner and Sara.

"I think you'll agree you two are fucked."

Sara gazed at the men, then at Liliya, who was smiling at her with a smug look.

"Matthews?"

"Yes, Miss Blake?"

"You're all going to die."

Tanner's smile was infinitesimal, but it was there. Sara Blake was one of the toughest women, hell, one of the toughest people he had ever known, and he was proud that she was his woman.

Now, he just had to think of a way to make Sara's words come true.

9
I AM NOT A MONKEY!

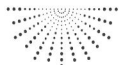

Matthews tore his eyes away from Sara and studied Tanner.

"You're Tanner."

"And you're Dan Matthews."

"That's right, and as you can see, Tanner, you have zero chance to win this fight."

"I met a man named Brian earlier who thought the same way. He's dead now."

Matthews gestured with his chin, to indicate Polina, who was peeking out from behind Tanner's back.

"Who's the little girl?"

"Red Riding Hood, we were taking her to see her grandmother."

Matthews sighed. "Ah, now I remember the phone conversations we had. You were an asshole then too, and arrogant."

"You came over here for a reason, Matthews," Tanner said, then he looked at Gleb. "Or were you taking your pet monkey for a walk?"

Gleb blinked several times in quick succession as a

scowl formed on his face. As dumb as he was, he did speak two languages, because his mother had been an Englishwoman. Although Gleb and Aleksandr spoke English, neither one of them could read or write the language.

"Were you talking about me?"

Tanner gave a little laugh. "You dressed the monkey up like a man and taught it to mimic speech like a parrot? That's impressive, Matthews."

Gleb held up the hand grenade. "See this? This is hand grenade. I could blow you to little bits."

Tanner was getting exactly the reaction he had wished for. He only hoped that Gleb was as stupid as he looked.

"That's a toy, Monkey man, anyone can see that."

"What did you call me?"

"Monkey man, and I bet they called you Monkey boy back when you went to school… *if* you went to school."

Polina stuck her head out farther to get a good look at Gleb, and yes, he did resemble an ape. Despite her fear, Polina giggled, then hid back behind Tanner.

When Gleb heard her laughter, he turned bright red and issued a string of Russian curses at Tanner.

Nikolai stepped forward and tried to get things back on track.

"Tanner, pay no attention to Smith, or Matthews, as you call him. My name is Nikolai. If you come with me, I promise not to hurt the woman or the little girl."

"But you'll kill me?"

Nikolai shrugged and waved a hand at the others. "You could shoot me and Matthews, but someone will kill you. There's no way for you to survive this many guns. But my way, you can be sure that your friends stay safe."

"It's a tempting offer, Nikolai, but what's to stop the

others from doing what they please? Are you saying you're in charge and not Matthews?"

Fedor stepped forward with Liliya on his arm. "I am in charge. My name is Fedor."

Tanner studied him and realized that he had been the pilot of the helicopter.

"You saw what I did to Brian and his crew, do you want some of the same?"

Fedor laughed. "You can't make like the fishy and swim behind us this time, Tanner."

"You can still strip down naked if you want to," Liliya said.

Tanner nodded toward Gleb. "Not in front of the monkey. He might get ideas."

"I am not a monkey!" Gleb shouted, as he shook the grenade at Tanner in warning. "My name is Gleb. Do not call me Monkey man."

The grenade was a Russian F1, with an average fuse time of only four seconds. The thing had a large blast radius as well. Tanner had run over all their options. Goading Gleb into using the grenade seemed their only chance, regardless of the degree of danger it posed.

"A monkey with a toy grenade," Tanner said. "Go wait in the plane, Monkey man; maybe you'll find a banana."

The tall biker, the one who hadn't lusted after Polina, smiled. Gleb saw it. It made him angrier and he yelled at the biker.

"Who are you smiling at, asshole?"

The biker pointed at Gleb. He spoke in broken English that gave away his Polish accent. "Is true. You look like monkey, but big monkey, like orangutan."

Tanner looked at Aleksandr. "You're his brother?"

"Da."

"How often do you have to shave him down?"

The biker laughed, but Matthews raised his hands and told everyone to shut up. Tanner couldn't have that, not when he was so close to pushing Gleb over the edge.

"Matthews, I know you wanted to intimidate me, but bringing along a phony grenade was too much."

Gleb placed a finger inside the pin. "Grenade is real, hit man."

"It's a toy," Tanner said. "Nothing but a toy, and even if it were real, you wouldn't have the balls to use it."

Gleb said, "Fuck you!" as he pulled the pin and slid the grenade toward Tanner.

Tanner rushed toward the grenade while shouting, "Get down!" to Sara and Polina. A second and a half after the pin was pulled, Tanner kicked the grenade back in the other direction. He watched it rocket away across the ice as he was diving to the ground.

His target wasn't Matthews and the others. He was sending the orb of death toward the larger group of men who were assembled near the planes.

When the grenade exploded, more than a dozen men cried out in pain, but, their cries went unheard. Their screams and howls of agony had been eclipsed by the strident sound of cracking ice, as a fissure opened between the two aircraft. The planes had both been struck by shrapnel, but the damage was cosmetic, other than a blown-out window. None of that mattered however, because as the fissure widened, the ice surrounding it weakened with a spider web of cracks, then collapsed into the water below.

A wing of the phony rescue plane slid into the gap first, but the other plane followed, and their weight widened the crevice. Both planes had been left running, and when the fuel tank of Nikolai's plane split open, aviation fuel spread across the ice.

Although farther away from the blast, Aleksandr had taken a tiny fragment to his shoulder, while the biker who had been leering at Polina was down on the ice and holding his leg, which was spurting blood.

Sara and Polina had been uninjured, as both had been lying flat, however, behind them, the snowmobile was sputtering. Tanner saw that shrapnel had damaged the snowmobile. It was leaking fluid.

"Sara, get on the snowmobile with Polina and ride back to the tent."

"What about you?"

"Just go!"

Polina opened her mouth to protest leaving Tanner, but Sara took her by the hand and pulled her toward the snowmobile.

Tanner held his rifle with one hand, while he used the other to reach into a pocket of the hoodie. No one was paying attention to him. They were all stunned by the drama of the planes entering the water and horrified by the screams of the injured men. They also realized that the loss of the planes had stranded them.

Many of the wounded were sliding into the water. Their howls of pain ended with sputtering sounds, as their lungs filled with the frigid liquid of the lake.

Nikolai was at Liliya's side, checking to see that she was uninjured by the blast. She was unharmed and complaining about her stylish blue boots, which had been stained by someone's blood.

The aviation fuel reached Matthews' party and spread around their feet. As the sound of the snowmobile's revving engine reverberated across the lake, all eyes turned to look at it.

"They're getting away!" Gleb said.

Apparently, he was the last one to notice that Tanner

was still in their midst. Tanner stood with the AK-47 in one hand, and a flare gun in the other. When Gleb finally spotted him, he smiled.

"I told you grenade was real."

"That you did," Tanner said, as he aimed the flare gun at Matthews' feet.

Nikolai looked down and saw that everyone but Tanner was standing in a layer of aviation fuel, including Liliya.

"Tanner no! You'll hurt my wife."

Tanner fired the flare gun. The flame was small one moment, then everywhere the next. Although frightening, the fire burned no higher than the tops of their shoes. If everyone stayed calm, many of them could have walked out of the fuel puddle before their clothing caught fire.

Everyone did not remain calm, especially after those who had been exposed to more of the fuel near the planes lit up like candles atop a birthday cake.

One of the bikers with Nikolai, the injured one who had leered at Polina, caught fire as he sat on the ice holding his wounded leg. When he attempted to push himself up, his hands slid on the ice, and he fell on his face, catching his hair on fire. By the time he crawled out of the flames, he had suffered severe burns that were life-threatening.

Meanwhile, in his panic to get to safety, Fedor had shoved past Liliya and caused her to trip and lose her balance. She was falling toward the flames when Nikolai grabbed her and lifted her, then he carried her to safety. Afterward, Liliya jumped out of his arms and ran to check on Fedor.

∽

One of Matthews' pant legs was on fire by the time he made it out of the burning fuel. He rolled in the snow near the lake's edge to put out the flames. One pant leg was ragged looking and singed up to the knee, but the flesh on his leg was only reddened, although it stung like hell. Matthews looked about and saw that Tanner was gone, and without doubt had sped off to rendezvous with Blake and the girl in a place of safety. A quick look around showed Matthews that they had suffered tremendous losses. Between his party and Nikolai's, they had landed on the lake with two dozen armed men.

On the other hand, Tanner had only Sara Blake and appeared handicapped by having to protect a child.

Only minutes had passed, and they were a ragtag group of seven survivors with no way to fly back to the city. Their supplies were in the lake along with the planes and night was approaching, to bring with it a snowstorm.

The sound of the snowmobile could be heard, but it was fading as Tanner and Sara Blake made their escape. Matthews looked over at Gleb. The idiot had tossed a live grenade without a thought to the damage it might do to anyone but Tanner. Not only did the man look simian, but he was about as smart as an ape too.

Matthews called to him, then spoke in Russian.

"Gleb."

"Huh?"

"Didn't you say you had three grenades?"

"The other two were in the plane."

"Too bad. I would love to shove one down Tanner's throat."

"I don't like him," Gleb said. "He's mean."

Matthews stood. His wet pants were turning to ice, while one side of them made him look as if he were wearing tattered shorts.

If they didn't find shelter or build a fire soon they'd all freeze to death. He recalled the campsite they spotted from the air, it was on the opposite shore, where the lake curved and ended in a cove.

"Follow me everyone, it's time to go lick our wounds."

Fedor opened his mouth to protest Matthews acting like their leader, but then shrugged.

The others tagged along behind Matthews, as on the lake, several men moaned and writhed in agony from either burns, wounds, or a combination of both.

Liliya gazed back as she asked a question. "Shouldn't someone put them out of their misery?"

No one answered her, and they walked on toward the campsite.

10

HOLE UP

Tanner rejoined Sara and Polina when they were still a short distance from the campsite.

Polina let out a squeal of joy when she saw Tanner and leapt into his arms, then she pecked him on the lips.

"You saved us by outsmarting that man, and he really does look like a monkey."

"You did good too. You got down low when you needed to, but why did you stop here?"

"The snowmobile died," Sara said. "I tried starting it, but I think the gas drained from it."

"I was afraid that would happen. We need to hide it. If Matthews and the others find it, they'll know that we're nearby. I want them to think we got away."

"How many are left?"

"I'm not certain, but it's less than ten. If this rifle wasn't so low on ammo and I had a spot to take cover, there wouldn't be that many left alive."

Polina pointed to the gun on his hip.

"Can you use the bullets from the gun inside the rifle?"

"They're not compatible."

"You mean they are different types?"

"Yes."

"I did not know that all bullets were not the same, but it makes sense, because the rifle is bigger."

Tanner stared at her and Polina grew nervous.

"Why are you looking at me like that?"

"I'm impressed by you. Many girls your age would be freaking out right now."

Polina grinned. "Freaking out, that means scared?"

"Yes."

"I am scared, but I know you will protect me."

"I will, and so will Sara. Now, let's hide this snowmobile and find shelter. It will be dark soon."

"Speaking of shelter," Sara said. "Where will we go?"

"I know the perfect spot."

POLINA HESITATED AS SHE STOOD AT THE LIP OF THE PIT and looked in, to see Sara staring up at her. The girl was frightened of reentering the pit, but Tanner assured her it would be all right.

"But… we will be trapped down there," Polina said.

"The lid is rigged so that we can open it at any time and I removed the lock."

"What if the men find us?"

"I placed tripwires in the area, so we'll know when someone's close by."

"I don't like the pit, Tanner."

"I know, but it will be warm thanks to the heated soapstone, and we'll have food and light."

"What about a bathroom? I may have to… tinkle."

"You'll have privacy, see, I placed the tent around the

toilet." Tanner leaned over and stared into Polina's eyes. "I thought you trusted me?"

"I do," Polina said. "But I'm still scared."

"I understand, but we have to get inside now. I can hear Matthews and the others coming."

Polina took a deep breath, released it, and climbed down the rope ladder. Tanner followed, pulled on a wire salvaged from the snowmobile, and the hatch that covered the pit closed.

There was light inside from the lantern, at least enough to see by. They opened another MRE, but only removed the crackers and cheese spread, since they had no way to heat the food.

The covering of the pit was thick and blocked most sounds from above, but Tanner guessed that Matthews and the others were up top and restarting the fire he'd put out earlier.

"Since we have nothing to do, tell me more about Genevieve," Sara said.

"Do you really want to hear that?"

"Tanner, you said a rapist was stalking the girl, but you never said what happened. I'm dying of curiosity."

"Who is Genevieve?" Polina asked.

"She was a girl Tanner knew when he was about your age and on a hunting trip with his grandfather. But Genevieve was in trouble when he left off the story."

Polina sat up straighter. "I love stories, and I want to hear about boy Tanner."

Sara grinned. "Yes, tell us about boy Tanner."

Tanner agreed. It would be a good way to keep Polina calm and help pass the time.

"Okay, like I said, Genevieve became friendly when she saw that I was a good shooter, but that changed after I bagged a deer, one of the large bucks."

"She was frightened of all the blood?" Polina said.
"Something like that."

Genevieve glanced back over her shoulder to make sure that no one was around before she unfastened her pants to pee. She did not like hunting. If her mother had told her she would have to pee out in the cold air with strangers around, she never would have agreed to come on the trip. After relieving herself, she used the toilet paper her mother had given her.

This is so gross, she thought, then wondered how the pioneers ever survived. As she was pulling her pants up, Genevieve heard a noise behind her. She turned her head and saw no one, but there was a tree there that was wide enough for someone to hide behind if they stood sideways.

She thought of the boy, Cody Parker, but when she left his side, Cody had been about to cut open a huge deer he'd killed with a single shot. The boy could shoot, that was for certain, and Genevieve was wondering if he were also a peeping Tom.

"Cody, is that you? It'd better not be. Hello, is anyone there?"

Nothing, only the breeze flowing through the brush and the pines. With her business done, Genevieve headed back toward the spot she'd left her mother and the Parkers, but then, she heard movement from behind, as a form rushed toward her.

Genevieve spun around so fast that she stumbled and fell backwards, to sit on a soft layer of snow. When the frightened deer flew by, it was a blur, but was so close that she could have touched it.

After placing her hand over her heart and laughing at

her own fright, Genevieve picked up her toilet paper and continued on her way.

Back in the trees, a face poked out from behind a wide pine, and in his hand, he held a knife.

Genevieve had expected to see the deer cut open when she returned, but the sight that greeted her both sickened and amazed her. Cody had sliced open the deer all right, and he was shoulder-deep inside the animal while his grandfather held the front legs of the poor creature. The boy was pulling at something for all he was worth. When it came free, the animal's organs spewed out with it. Cody had been gripping the buck's windpipe, and he pulled it free like the stem on an apple.

"Ooh, that is so gross," Genevieve said.

Cody stared at her, as he stood amid the deer's innards. "This is called field dressing, Genevieve. It has to be done to protect the meat from getting bacteria."

"It's sick! And… to do that, to just reach inside and… you're a monster, Cody. And hunting sucks."

Genevieve ran back toward base camp with her mother following.

"Genevieve!" Cody called, but it was useless.

Polina was making a face of disgust. "Hunting sounds nasty."

Sara laughed at Tanner's story. "I was grossed out the first time I saw someone field strip a deer too, but since then, I've seen autopsies performed."

"Genevieve was not pleased with me," Tanner said.

Polina stretched out on the mattress and laid her head on Tanner's lap. "Finish the story tomorrow, Tanner. Right now, I need to close my eyes." The girl was so tired that she fell asleep in seconds.

Sara smiled at her. "If she were a little older, I'd be jealous."

"She is a beauty."

"Speaking of teenage beauties, did Genevieve ever speak to you again? And what about the creep that was stalking her?"

Tanner was about to answer Sara when they heard raised voices drift down from above.

"It sounds like the neighbors aren't getting along," Tanner said.

"I hope they kill each other," Sara said.

"I could slip up there in the dark and help them along."

"Let's deal with them when we don't have to worry about protecting Polina. Our priority should be to get this child to safety."

Tanner looked down at the girl. "I agree, for now."

THE LOUD VOICE THEY HEARD BELONGED TO FEDOR, WHO had been shouting at Dan Matthews. Matthews had told Fedor to gather fresh firewood and Fedor took offense at being told what to do. From there, the group had split into two factions. Matthews, Gleb, Aleksandr, and Nikolai made up one group, while the tall biker, who went by the name Boz, sided with Fedor and Liliya.

"The way I look at it, Smith, you owe me for the plane I lost, no, two planes, Nikolai's plane is ruined too."

Matthews laughed at Fedor. "Sue me for it. You can tell

a judge how things went wrong when we were hunting down a man to kill him."

Fedor smirked. "Tanner called you Matthews. That means you changed your name for a reason. I bet the law would be interested in knowing why."

They went back and forth like that and no one noticed when Nikolai disappeared. However, they did react to the flare of light when the fire began and looked over to see that Nikolai had started a blaze.

As they joined him around the fire, Nikolai spoke.

"We can't fight each other. If we do, we only hurt ourselves. I say we get some sleep and then move out at dawn. I'll take the first watch, and Smith, you take the second, Fedor, take the third. Tanner might still be around."

"You don't tell me what to do, Nikolai," Fedor said. "I'll take the first watch."

"I don't care, Fedor, I only care about finding Tanner and killing him."

"Nikolai," Liliya said. "Tanner is gone. Don't you remember? He had a snowmobile."

"I remember seeing that thing leaking some sort of fluid like a sieve after the grenade went off. Tanner didn't get far, and I doubt he's traveling in the dark with that little girl. Come first light, I'm going to look for him and I'm going to kill him."

"That's crazy," Fedor said. "We have no supplies and a snowstorm is coming."

"Do what you want, Fedor, but I'm going to kill Tanner."

"Why Nikolai?" Liliya asked.

"Because he nearly killed you. He knew you were standing in fuel and he set it on fire. I'll kill him for that."

"We'll both kill him," Matthews said. "If I leave him

alive, he'll hunt me down someday. I might as well finish it now."

Gleb pounded a fist on his knee. "We'll all kill Tanner, and then we'll be famous."

Nikolai lay on the ground beside the fire. "I don't care about anything except killing Tanner, but I do need some sleep. Fedor, wake me in a few hours."

Less than an hour later, they were all asleep.

11

WHAT THE MIND HEARS, THE HEART IGNORES

Pavel entered a restaurant in the city of Barnaul and looked around for his dinner companion, his sister, Valentina.

He spotted her sitting at the bar and nursing a vodka martini. He had arrived on time but spent the last fifteen minutes being certain he wasn't walking into a trap. The dinner meeting wasn't part of the plan, and any deviation from the plan worried Pavel.

He trusted Valentina, and only Valentina, who, although just six years older than Pavel, had raised him when their parents died. Still, she might have been followed without knowing, and it paid to be cautious.

They were not born with the names Pavel and Valentina but given them out of necessity. When Valentina was fourteen and Pavel was eight, their parents sat them down at the kitchen table and told them that their lives were about to change forever.

Their parents admitted that they had been involved in a conspiracy to overthrow the Russian government. They told them that the authorities would discover that truth within hours and that they were not going to run or hide.

They had decided to kill themselves. Pavel and Valentina's parents knew too much about many people, people who could keep the revolution alive until the time was right to change the world. Were they to be taken alive and tortured, they would be forced to betray their friends. They would die by their own hands before they let that happen.

Those same friends would take care of Pavel and Valentina, would protect them, and guide them, so that someday they too could help the cause and hasten the revolution.

After their parents' deaths, Valentina became a fervent revolutionary, although she kept her passion well-concealed from those in authority. Pavel was also dedicated to their cause, and had joined the Russian army, where he and others infiltrated the military.

More than twenty years had passed since their parents killed themselves, and Valentina was a leader in their organization. Although she tried to be patient, she found it difficult. Valentina developed a bold plan to grab power in a matter of weeks instead of years, and the kidnapping of Polina was a part of that plan.

PAVEL APPROACHED HIS SISTER WHILE STUDYING HER, TO gauge her mood. Valentina was good-looking with her long dark hair and trim, shapely figure. But there was something in her manner that let you know she didn't want to talk, and no man had approached her or offered to buy her a drink.

Valentina had always radiated aloofness, Pavel knew,

even as a child. It was a byproduct of her intellect. One part of her mind was always working, always thinking ahead.

The kidnapping and assassinations that had taken place during the day would ensure that the Russia of the future would be more to their liking, and that their own people would be sitting in seats of power.

Pavel thought of Polina again and felt regret. The girl was an innocent, but the short time of fear she would live through, along with her death, would have meaning over the coming years. Valentina, himself, and the others who served the cause did so out of love, not evil. The revolution they served was much like the labor experienced by a mother. The new being was only born after much pain.

Pavel greeted Valentina with a kiss on the cheek, then kept the conversation light until they were seated at a table. Once they were alone with their meals ordered, Pavel took several gulps from his beer before asking the question that was uppermost in his mind.

"Is there a problem?"

Valentina smiled. "The two assassinations went off without incident and both shooters died bravely, while all evidence points toward Muslim extremists."

Pavel drained the rest of his beer. When he looked for their waiter, he saw the man talking with one of the barmaids. Pavel gritted his teeth in irritation. He was a soldier in the revolution and he had dedicated his life to being the best at everything he did. However, most people, such as his waiter, were lackadaisical about their work and responsibilities.

It was Pavel's belief that everyone should not only serve a tour in the military, where they would learn discipline, but should also practice martial arts. In the arena, if you were lax in your training, you paid for it. There was no latitude in combat. You performed well, or you suffered.

His ability to commit, to dedicate himself to a purpose, was just one of the reasons that Pavel was deadly at hand-to-hand combat. He understood what it took to be a master of anything. Mastery demanded that you follow the rules, that you keep improving, and that you take things seriously. Pavel was a master of his chosen discipline, Combat Sambo. It had been years since he'd suffered defeat. He would match his technique and skills against anyone.

After failing to catch the waiter's eye, Pavel turned his attention back to Valentina. "The authorities are always ready to blame the Muslims for any act of terror. But what about our kidnapping demands, has there been any progress made there?"

"Your abduction of Polina has made her grandmother agree to our terms."

"The old bitch agreed already? That is good. I thought we would have to harm the child first?"

"No, as I told you, the woman loves Polina more than anything. Once we prove to her that Polina is well, she will go on live TV, admit to treason, and resign, which will open the way for our man to take her position."

Pavel smiled, as his mood brightened.

The waiter brought their food. While glaring at the man, Pavel asked him for another beer. The man returned his glare with a plastic smile and walked over to talk to the barmaid again. Pavel cut into his steak, as he waited for his second drink to arrive, but the waiter just kept on talking and laughing with the barmaid. As Pavel sighed in exasperation, a thought occurred to him.

"Valentina, you could have spoken to me in code over the phone. Something else is on your mind."

"We need money, Pavel. Revolutions are fueled by passion, but funded by rubles."

"Isn't that why we entered the drug trade?"

"It is, but defending ourselves against other dealers and the cost of bribery eat up a large percentage of the profit. We need another stream of income, and I have found one that involves little risk."

"Such as?"

"White slavery, and the girl, Polina, she will be our first transaction."

Pavel was about to respond when a miracle occurred. The waiter had returned with his beer, which he sat on the table, while spilling some, of course. As the waiter walked away, Pavel responded to Valentina's last statement.

"You want to sell the girl? But, Valentina, she has seen me and the Turks."

"It doesn't matter. Where Polina is going, no one will care about or listen to anything she says. Her family's wealth and status will be meaningless. She'll be a sex slave for a man who could buy and sell her entire family."

Pavel drank half of his second beer, sat the mug on the table, and gave the proposition some thought.

"How much will we get for the girl?"

Valentina said a figure and Pavel looked doubtful. "Why so much money for one girl?"

"You've seen her, she is beautiful, blonde, and a virgin. At least, she'd better still be a virgin. If the Turks touched her I will kill them myself."

"The Turks are not the type to rape. If she was a virgin, she has remained one."

"That girl has never known a man, trust me, I can tell."

Pavel decided that he agreed with Valentina's new plan. He finished cutting his steak, took a bite, and found that it was excellent. After eating in silence for a few moments, Pavel made an observation about the change in plans.

"At least this way, the girl will live. I was not looking forward to killing her."

"Yes, but these new partners, they are as dangerous as the men we buy our drugs from. If we do not deliver Polina in two days, there will be severe consequences."

"You mean they will try to kill us?"

"Exactly, but they'll also pay us for any other girls we bring them of a similar quality."

Pavel groaned. "The things we do for revolution, trafficking in little girls for perverts. It's sickening."

"I agree, but we promised ourselves a long time ago that we would let nothing get in our way, not even our own sense of right and wrong. If something advances our cause, then, it is right. In the end, we will honor mother and father."

Pavel went back to eating as Valentina did the same, but she was a vegetarian, and rarely ate more than small portions. Several minutes after Valentina had finished her meal, Pavel pushed his empty plate aside.

"When I see the girl tomorrow, I'll make sure that she's treated better after I make the video of her we need. Where will the exchange take place?"

"Where she is now, at the lake. They'll arrive on a helicopter."

Pavel wrinkled his brow, as those arrangements surprised him. "There is a blizzard coming. They say we're getting over two feet of snow tomorrow. Most helicopters can't land in two feet of snow."

"If it's not feasible then they will arrive on snowmobiles and take her to the aircraft. Cover your face if you'd like, but I gave them your name. Pavel is a common enough name. There will be two men, while you and the Turks will be three. I expect no difficulties; these are professionals. You give them the girl and they'll give you the money in cash. It will be euros, not rubles."

"All right, and we can certainly use the money."

Valentina held up her glass for a toast. "It is finally happening, Pavel. A new Russia is on the horizon."

Pavel clinked his mug against her glass. There was nothing that could stop them now.

While flying in a private jet toward Barnaul, Russia, Jacques Durand went over the latest reports out of Moscow. The two assassinations were disturbing enough, given that the victims were both members of The Russian Federation Council. However, the kidnapping of another member's granddaughter hinted at a devious mind at work. If the woman gave in to the kidnapper's demands, it would ruin not only her reputation, but taint those around her. That was why she too hadn't been murdered, ruining the woman would accomplish far more.

Although his agency wasn't involved with the hunt for the kidnappers, Durand had asked to be kept apprised of any developments. He tossed the reports onto the empty seat beside him and looked at the setting sun. His mind wasn't on work, but rather, was filled with thoughts of a personal nature.

Sara Blake was missing, as the small plane she and Tanner had been on never arrived at its destination.

Search planes had flown over the missing aircraft's most likely course but had discovered nothing.

Durand felt his phone vibrate and discovered he had a text from a contact in Barnaul. The text informed him that a group of Australian mercenaries were said to have gone after Tanner. When the helicopter returned without the mercs, a much larger group went after him, but had yet to return.

Durand phoned his contact, a man named Karl, and asked for more details.

"There aren't any specifics, Jacques. And understand, I got most of this secondhand from a topless dancer. It seems her bosses were on one of the other planes."

"Planes? How many men went after Tanner?"

"At least twenty, but maybe more. I hate to say it, but I guess we just lost an asset."

"I don't like Tanner, but he is resourceful. It's Sara Blake I'm concerned about."

"Listen, Jacques, I'd like to do more, but they have me helping out on that kidnapping."

"I thought that happened in Novosibirsk?"

"It did, but one of the dead assassins was traced to Barnaul. Facial recognition tied him to footage taken by CCTV cameras."

"I'm not familiar with the area, Karl, what is south of Barnaul?"

"There are a few small communities, but it's mostly open land."

"That sounds like a good place to ambush someone."

"You're talking about Tanner and Blake, but I thought they were headed north?"

"That's what I thought too, now I'm not so sure. Maybe the search planes were looking in the wrong area. Thank you, Karl, and good luck finding your kidnapped girl."

"Thanks, and good luck to you too."

Durand ended the call and took out his laptop to look up a map of the area south of Barnaul. Karl had been correct. There were a few towns, and toward the southeast, there was only wilderness.

Durand checked the weather forecast for the area and cursed when he saw how bad the storm was expected to be. It would not only make conditions brutal for anyone without shelter but would also keep search planes grounded.

It didn't matter, he decided, one way or another, he would search for Sara Blake. He cared for her too much to just sit on his hands and do nothing.

"The woman is involved with someone and damn near half your age," he whispered to himself, and while his mind listened, his heart paid no attention.

12

SENSELESS VIOLENCE

The following morning, inside the pit, Tanner readied the rifle as one of his tripwires was tugged. The "wire" was a single strand of rope. It was attached to two of the empty tin cans from the MRE, and they rattled together in warning.

Polina had been asleep, but when the jangling cans woke her, she scurried across the mattress and into Sara's arms.

"They have found us," Polina said in Russian. Sara didn't speak the language, but understood the girl's meaning, and felt her tremble.

Sara hugged the girl. "We'll be fine, Polina. There's a chance it's just animals of some type."

Tanner had been listening with his head cocked. "They are animals, maybe the wolves we've been hearing. I can make out several of them padding across the cover of the pit. They had stopped to sniff at the lid of the pit, but they're moving on."

"We have big wolves in Russia, Tanner, but they don't attack," Polina said, in English.

"The problem is, they're headed toward the campsite. Those fools might shoot at them if they spot them."

The words had barely left Tanner's mouth when the gunfire began. Tanner climbed up the rope ladder and opened the lid over the pit enough to climb out. As he did so, fresh snow drifted in, along with sparse daylight and a rush of cold air.

"Can you see anything?" Sara asked.

"No, but I can hear that idiot, Gleb. He's bragging about having shot three of the wolves."

"Oh no, they kill the wolves?" Polina said.

"They're saying one got away, and Matthews is telling them to move out."

After brushing away his tracks, Tanner climbed back inside the pit and closed the lid.

"We'll give them a few minutes to leave and then we'll eat. Afterward, we'll follow their footprints north. I'm sure they believe we're in front of them."

Tanner checked out the area before telling Sara and Polina to climb out of the pit. Along the shoreline, he found several wolves that had been shot to death. The thickening snow had already coated their bodies.

The fire had still been burning, causing Tanner to wonder if perhaps Matthews and his companions were planning to return. But, no, the careless fools had neglected to put out the flames. In a way, it was good, they could heat their own food faster.

Polina went up the rope ladder with no problem, but it was a struggle for Sara. Her knee had swollen overnight, and it hurt each time she bent it.

"Maybe I should leave you and Polina inside the pit while I go get help," Tanner said.

"No. I'm sick of being down there, and my knee will be fine. Although, I'll need to move slower than yesterday, especially in this snow."

Polina wept when she spotted the wolves, who were nearly as large as she was. She then pointed at the ground. "A set of paw prints lead into the trees. One of the wolves did get away."

After they'd eaten, Sara angrily tossed snow onto the fire. "The idiots! Killing wolves for no reason. I hope they become lost and freeze to death out here."

"They may not get the chance," Tanner said, and Sara took his meaning.

Polina seemed subdued. She missed her family and worried about what they might be thinking happened to her. She also kept looking behind, as if she expected someone to be following them.

"You're worried about the man who flew you here, aren't you?" Tanner said.

"I think he is like you, very tough."

"I hope he shows," Tanner said.

"Why?" Polina asked. "So you can fight him?"

"No, but the weather is too bad to fly in, so that means he'll have a snowmobile, which means *we'll* have a snowmobile. If that happens, you'll be back with your family faster."

"That man frightens me, Tanner. He said he killed Stas, and Stas was very tough."

"Tough in what way, was he a boxer?"

"Stas knew karate, judo, and he carried a gun too."

"It sounds like the man that took you may be into martial arts as well."

Polina wiped away tears. "He said he broke Stas' neck."

Tanner filed that away as a reminder not to take the man lightly, whoever he was.

THE MAN'S NAME WAS PAVEL KRASOTKIN. PAVEL RODE HIS snowmobile into the area and decided to cut across the lake. When he came upon the two airplanes mostly submerged beneath a thin layer of new ice, Pavel wondered what mayhem had taken place during his absence. Surely the planes hadn't both crashed in the same spot.

None of the snow-coated corpses scattered across the lake belonged to the two Turks, and there was no trace of them at the campsite, nor of the girl, Polina. The pit puzzled him. Why bring the tent down inside it or rig it to be opened from within?

Finding the dead wolves saddened Pavel, as he had always admired the creatures, while the missing snowmobile had Pavel thinking the Turks had ridden off with the girl. Perhaps, upon seeing the strangers arrive in the planes, they thought it best to move to the secondary location.

The backup site consisted of decrepit old buildings abandoned after World War II. The tent offered better shelter from the storm than did those crumbling wood buildings, still, they might hide them from the view of strangers in planes.

While coming back from the pit, Pavel searched the area and found the snowmobile. The vehicle had been deliberately hidden and showed signs of damage by a projectile of some sort. The gas tank was empty, and it had been nearly full. That was bad, as Pavel had planned to siphon fuel from the machine to use for his trip back. He cursed himself for not filling up his tank before leaving, but he'd been so eager to film the girl, in order to offer her grandmother Proof of Life.

There was a hill nearby. Pavel scrambled up to the top of it and used the scope on his rifle to search. He gazed south, saw no sign that the snow had been disturbed, then moved the scope northward, as he looked for movement or shoe prints.

He spotted them walking along a path in the lowland, amid the trees, and caught a good look at the group once they strode through a small clearing. They were a party of six men, while the seventh figure appeared to be the girl, Polina. Pavel was too far away to make out facial features, but he saw a petite form and blonde hair. His mind raced. If the strangers had the girl, then where were the Turks?

Dead, they were dead, and the girl taken by the others.

Could this be the white slavers? Pavel thought. *Maybe they came a day early and decided to take the girl without paying.*

But no, one of the aircraft in the water had the markings of a rescue plane. But they couldn't have been looking for the girl, and since when do rescue workers carry guns? It was all perplexing, except for one fact. Pavel had to get the girl back. If that meant he had to kill everyone with her, then so be it.

He had a satellite phone on his hip. The sophisticated device would work even during a snowstorm. Valentina told him it was to be used only for an emergency. Pavel thought this situation qualified as one.

When Valentina answered, Pavel heard both concern and annoyance in her tone.

"What is the problem?"

Pavel filled her in on the situation and heard silence on the other end. He waited. He was aware of Valentina's ways and knew the silence meant that she was thinking things through and conjuring, sorting, then discarding possibilities. When she was certain of a response, then she would speak.

"It's the buyers. They must be trying to take the girl early and cheat us."

"Why would they bring two planes for one girl?"

"It's possible they collided in the storm with the rescue plane and came down together on a lake that couldn't support the planes combined weight."

Pavel looked out at the lake and doubted that scenario. The planes appeared to be too close together.

"I don't think that is what occurred, but it is a puzzling scene. One thing we do know, the girl is gone, and a group of armed men have her."

"If you give me a few hours I can have two men there to help you, Bogdan and Ruslan."

"Bogdan and Ruslan? They have no experience with something like this. No, I will handle the situation myself."

"Are you certain, Pavel? I know your skills, but I worry."

Pavel smiled. "It's because of my skills and training that you don't need to worry. I will get the girl back and call you by sundown."

"Good, but keep Polina alive. I know of another buyer for her in South America. The price they'll pay is less, but at least they won't kill our men and cheat us."

"These buyers, Valentina, are you in danger from them?"

"One of them knows my face, that is all."

"I'll deal with them in time, for now, I must catch up with the ones who have taken the girl."

"Be careful, Pavel, and don't forget to call."

"I'll get the girl back, count on it."

In Barnaul, Jacques Durand was frustrated. There were lots of people with private planes and helicopters, but no one would risk going up during the snowstorm. Meanwhile, Sara was out there somewhere, possibly injured, freezing, and without food.

He'd decided to rent a snowmobile but was told they were all taken. When the gray-haired clerk asked him why he was going out in the middle of a storm, Durand told him it was to look for a friend who might be hurt. Durand's Russian was excellent, as he had worked in the country many years earlier.

"I believe my friend went down in that missing plane," Durand said.

"You're talking about Yaromir's plane? I heard about that. He went down with a young couple, are they your friends?"

"Yes, and I think people have been looking in the wrong area for them. I think the plane may have gone down south of here."

"Have you ridden a snowmobile before?"

"I know how they work."

"The storm will only get worse. No one should be out there in the wilderness alone."

"I would normally agree, but I'm willing to risk it."

The clerk thought that over, then, he made a hand gesture that told Durand to wait for a second. When the clerk picked up the land line phone, Durand wondered who the man was calling.

After a conversation that Durand couldn't quite hear, the clerk hung up and smiled at him.

"My friend Sasha will take you out to look, but it won't be cheap."

"Does she know the area well?"

"She's a native. You couldn't get her lost if you tried."

"Excellent, and I'll be glad to pay. But tell me, what sort of plane does she have?"

"Oh, I never said she had a plane."

"A snowmobile?"

The clerk smiled. "You're getting closer."

"A DOG SLED?"

Sasha Anovso-Roberts grinned at Durand. She was a Russian Eskimo in her twenties, a Yupik, and her long dark hair framed a pretty face. Durand stood outside her kennel and watched the excited dogs yelp and play together. The snow had increased, and the world was becoming a showcase of white.

"Dogs are the best way to get around, Mr. Durand. And pardon the pun, but these puppies can move up to twelve miles an hour."

"You've spent time in the United States, haven't you?"

"Yes sir, I went to school at San Diego State, fell in love with an American geologist, and when his company transferred him, I wound up right back here in Barnaul. Fate can be funny that way."

"And cruel as well, which is why I need to find my friend."

"I thought we were looking for two people, three actually, counting old man Yaromir."

"Yes, three, but I'm most concerned about the young woman. Her name is Sara."

"Say the word. I'll saddle up the dogs and we'll be on our way."

Durand looked at the sled with trepidation. As he considered things, a girl walked over to hand Sasha a cloth bag. The girl was the niece of Sasha's husband. Her name was Brenda. She was sixteen, white, and had strawberry-blonde hair. Durand exchanged smiles with her, then pointed at the sled as he spoke to Sasha.

"How will I stay on that thing?"

Sasha grinned. "You'll be sitting while I stand behind you and steer. It's fun, you'll see."

"Yes, let's do it. This storm will only get worse."

"That price I gave you, that's paid up front."

"Of course, but tell me, what will we do if we find them?"

"I'll bring back anyone who's injured and leave the others with supplies and an emergency beacon. When the storm breaks overnight, they'll send out a larger rescue team, or maybe a chopper."

"You've done this sort of thing before?"

"Twice, both were small plane crashes out in the wild."

"Any survivors?"

"I'm sorry, Mr. Durand, but no, there weren't. But that doesn't mean there won't be this time."

"Sara's alive, and the man she's with… it would take a lot to kill him."

"He sounds like quite the man."

Durand frowned. "He's like no one you've ever met."

13
SOMEONE KIDNAPPED MY KIDNAP VICTIM

Matthews' ragtag group trudged along a crude path that wound through the forest.

Liliya complained about her feet hurting and how hungry she was, but of the seven of them, she was the only one who had eaten since the debacle on the lake. Nikolai had given her the protein bar he had in his jacket pocket.

Nikolai's cousin, Volya, never liked Liliya. She had offered to sleep with him once during her marriage to Nikolai, and Volya thought of her as a whore.

When Liliya announced that she had to take a break from the trek to urinate, two of the men decided to go as well. Volya and the biker named Boz walked into the trees on the right, while Liliya wandered off into the trees on the left.

Volya had grown up in Barnaul, while Boz had been raised in Warsaw, Poland. They had both grown up in cities, and so neither of them took much notice of the animal tracks marring the mounting snow.

Volya was wearing a long, black wool scarf. After unzipping, he saw that the scarf hung in the way. He removed it and stuffed it in his pocket. It had been making his beard itch. Anyway, he felt sufficiently warmed by all the walking he was doing.

Behind Volya, Boz was talking about how he would handle Tanner the next time he saw him. When Volya let out a wild scream of fright. Boz jerked around to look at him, and sprayed urine as he did so.

A large wolf had Volya pinned to the ground. The wolf's growling was ferocious, as was its attack. It snarled as it tore chunks of flesh from Volya's face and neck.

Boz ran away while zipping up his fly and looking over his shoulder. He covered twenty yards before he tripped over a tree root that was hidden beneath the snow. When Boz made it to his feet again, he ran smack into the hulking Gleb, bounced off, and fell onto his butt.

"What's going on?" Nikolai said. "Where's Volya?"

Boz pointed frantically as he rose again, but his words couldn't be understood because he was speaking his native Polish.

Nikolai took him by the shoulders. "In Russian, man, speak in Russian. Is it Tanner? Is he back?"

"No, Nikolai, it was a wolf, that huge wolf that survived the shooting this morning. Volya… oh man, Volya is dead, chewed up."

Nikolai released Boz's shoulders only to take him by the arm. "Show me where."

"What if the wolf is still there?"

"I'll shoot it."

"Shoot it?" Boz murmured, then wondered why the thought had never occurred to him. But, he knew why. He'd been so scared that all he could think about was running for safety.

Boz led the way and Nikolai let out a moan when he spotted the body. Volya's throat was ripped open, and half his face was missing, while bloody paw prints in the snow led off into the brush.

With a scream of anguish, Nikolai held the short Serbu shotgun at shoulder level, then aimed downward in the direction of the paw prints. When he had expended all three rounds, he leaned against a tree and cried.

"No, Volya, no."

There was silence for several seconds, but Gleb broke it with a question.

"Where is Liliya? She must have heard all the noise."

Nikolai's grief evaporated, to be replaced by worry. He and the others called for Liliya, but only the soft sound of falling snow answered their cries.

TANNER, SARA, AND POLINA, STOPPED WALKING WHEN THEY heard Nikolai shooting.

"That sounded close," Sara said. "No more than a mile."

Tanner loosened the straps on the backpack, removed it, and handed it to Polina. Sara's knee was getting worse, and the less weight she had to put on it, the better.

"I'm going to scout ahead and check that out. I want you two to get behind those large trees on the left there and wait for me to come back."

"I want to go with you," Polina said.

"No. You stay with Sara and do what she says. If someone approaches, you won't be hard to find in the snow, so there's no point in hiding, but the trees offer some cover."

"Can I have a gun?" Polina asked.

"Have you ever shot a gun?"

"When I was younger, Stas let me hold his empty gun. I remember it was heavy."

"I don't think giving you a gun is a good idea, Polina. You need training first."

Polina's shoulders slumped. "Can I at least have a knife?"

Tanner reached inside the backpack and removed a Ka-Bar knife in a sheath. Polina's eyes glittered at the sharpness of the weapon.

"You'll wear that on your belt, but don't use it unless you need to. It's very sharp and dangerous."

"Thank you, Tanner, for not treating me like a baby. And I use knives often in Girl Scouts."

Tanner kissed Sara. "I'll be back, and you'll hear me whistle first."

"Be careful," Sara said.

Tanner moved off into the trees on the left and was soon out of sight.

Polina appeared worried as she gazed in the direction Tanner had traveled.

"What if he doesn't come back?"

"That's not possible," Sara said.

Polina kept staring, then she smiled. "Da, he will be back. He is Tanner."

"Exactly," Sara said.

Liliya wanted to shout to the others as they called to her, but if she did, she was sure the man holding the knife to her throat would kill her.

Pavel had grabbed her from behind and kept her mouth covered so she wouldn't cry out. He thought he had been abducting Polina for the second time and was surprised when he spun Liliya around and saw he had a woman, and not a girl.

On the other hand, Liliya was certain she had been grabbed from behind by Tanner, and was equally shocked to see Pavel.

"Who are you?" Pavel asked in a whisper.

Liliya answered him in kind, by breathlessly saying her name.

"You were on one of the planes?"

"We came here to find a man. His name is Tanner."

"Who is he?"

"A hit man. They say he killed Maurice Scallato."

"Scallato?" Pavel said, but then he remembered the recent story about the assassin who murdered his own family in Sicily. He also recalled that Maurice Scallato was considered to have been one of the most dangerous men alive. If this Tanner killed Scallato, he would be formidable.

"I have friends looking for me. Hear them?"

"Who are they?"

"My boyfriend and my ex-husband. Oh, and his cousin and a man named Smith. There's also Gleb and Aleksandr, and they have money, they can pay you."

"Pay me for what?"

"For me. Let me go and they'll pay you."

"Have you seen a girl? She's about your size."

"Tanner has her, and there's a woman too."

"Tanner has the girl, then tell me what she looks like."

"Like you said, she's my size. Oh, and her hair is in pigtails. I think she's a little old for pigtails, but she is cute."

"And this Tanner, what does he look like?"

"His eyes, they're so intense, I've never seen eyes like that. Maybe that's what happens when you kill a lot of people, maybe it shows in the eyes."

"But, is he tall, short, thin, fat?"

"He, he's built like you, but taller. He's trim, but muscular. Even bundled up like he was, I could tell he was in shape... but those eyes. You'll know him when you see him."

Pavel put the knife away and unslung the shotgun he had. "And you say your name is Liliya?"

"Yes."

"Call your friends over here, Liliya, but then don't move. If you attempt to run away I will kill you."

"Please don't hurt me. I just want to get home."

"Do as I say and that might happen."

Pavel backed away from her and Liliya called for Fedor. It was Nikolai who answered, and Liliya called out again.

"I'm over here!"

Once Pavel knew what direction they would approach from, he hid and waited for their arrival. He had no plans to kill them... yet. They were going to help him find Polina.

TANNER HEARD LILIYA'S VOICE. SHE WAS CLOSE, AND didn't sound injured, more like fearful of something, or someone. After seeing footprints leading off into the trees, he followed them and came across Volya's body.

The lone wolf that survived the massacre was out for revenge, but Tanner knew the beast would attack any human he saw, given a chance. He thought about going back to warn Sara about the wolf but realized it wouldn't matter. Sara would be ready for anything that came her way, man or beast.

Before leaving, Tanner checked Volya's pockets for useful items. They still had two of the Russian MRE's and sticks of beef jerky, but food was too precious to leave behind. When he found the black scarf in Volya's pocket, he took it to give to Polina.

Moving away from Volya's body, Tanner followed in the footprints made by Matthews and the others. Only a tracker would know he hadn't been just another member of the group, and it paid to make as few fresh tracks as possible.

At the rate the snow was falling, all the shoe and boot prints would be covered up quickly. As they headed out that morning, Tanner had assumed they would be making better time, but the ground was uneven, the mounting snow was blinding, and Sara's knee was only getting worse.

When he returned to Sara and Polina, Tanner decided he would need to find shelter, but first, he had to reassess their situation.

Something had changed, he could feel it. Perhaps it was the wolf, but Polina's abductor may have come back, found her missing, and gone looking for her.

Given the size of Matthews' group, the man must have spotted them first.

After hearing voices ahead, including one he didn't recognize, Tanner slowed his pace, lowered himself into a crouch, and moved forward with stealth, like the assassin he was.

14

LONE WOLF

Nikolai pushed Fedor aside so he could reach Liliya first. She was frightened, that was obvious, but of what?

"Did the wolf attack you, Liliya?" Nikolai asked.

"What wolf? One of those damn wolves is around?"

Nikolai hung his head. "The thing killed Volya."

"Volya's dead? But no, never mind that, we have another problem."

"Tanner?" Fedor asked.

Liliya pointed to the last spot where she'd seen Pavel, and everyone turned to look. As they did so, Pavel came up behind Nikolai and placed a knife to his throat.

"If anyone points their weapon at me I will kill this man," Pavel said.

Fedor looked amused. "Go ahead, slit his throat and see if anyone cares."

Pavel realized his error, shoved Nikolai to the ground and grabbed Liliya. The amusement left Fedor's face and he pleaded with Pavel.

"Leave her alone."

"I don't want to harm her. I only want to get your attention."

"Who are you?" Matthews asked.

Pavel was going to make up a phony name, then decided it didn't matter. He would kill all of them, or the fools would die in the storm. Anyway, as Valentina had pointed out the previous evening, Pavel was a common name.

"I am Pavel, and I want you to help me kill Tanner. The child with him belongs to me."

Nikolai stood, then spoke as he wiped snow off his clothes. "What do you mean the girl belongs to you? Is she your daughter?"

"We became separated yesterday. Tanner must have found her."

"So, she is your daughter?"

Pavel ignored Nikolai and looked at the others as he spoke. "We must work together to kill Tanner."

"Tanner is gone," Fedor said. "He rode out of here yesterday on a snowmobile."

"Not true," Pavel said. "I found that machine hidden in the woods. Tanner is still on foot, and he must be close. Work with me and we can kill him."

"He could still be ahead of us," Matthews said.

Pavel shook his head. "Have you seen any other footprints in the snow? No, because he must be traveling behind you. If we work as one, we'll trap him."

"Let Liliya go and we'll listen to your plan," Nikolai said.

Pavel released her and Liliya went to Fedor.

"My plan is simple," Pavel said. "I chase Tanner toward you, and you kill him."

Gleb smiled. "I like that plan."

Tanner eased away from the group. He had heard enough and had a plan of his own. When he returned to the spot where he'd left Sara and Polina, he did so by making a wide arc and coming up behind them. He saw Sara relax when he whistled at his approach, and Polina greeted him with a short hug.

"There's a new player in the game. The man who kidnapped Polina, and he's sharp."

"What is his name, do you know?" Polina asked.

"He called himself Pavel."

Polina took out her knife. "I would like to stick this in Pavel for killing Stas."

"Keep that anger, Polina, it's more useful than fear. But if I have my way, we'll avoid Pavel altogether."

"What's the plan," Sara asked.

Tanner pointed at their earlier footprints, which were almost completely covered by the falling snow.

"Pavel wants to herd us toward Matthews and the others until we're trapped between them, but if we head east, back toward the ridge, I'm thinking they won't see our fresh tracks."

Sara frowned as she looked east. The terrain was steeper in that direction and it would tax her injured knee more.

Tanner took her gloved hand. "I know walking that way will be tougher for you, but I think there's a prize at the end."

"What prize?" Sara asked.

"Pavel didn't walk back here, and he couldn't have flown in this storm. He must have a snowmobile. If I can find the tracks it made and follow them, we could ride out of here and be back in Barnaul in no time."

"I'd love that," Sara said. "But what if Pavel approached us from the west?"

"The land to the west is lower. I'm thinking that Pavel tracked Matthews and his people by looking down on them from that eastern ridge."

"Yes, I can see that."

"Polina, please help Sara when we get to steeper ground."

Polina took Sara's hand. "Sara is my friend, of course I help her."

"There's one more thing," Tanner said, and then he told them about the wolf that killed Volya.

"The poor thing," Polina said. "He saw his whole pack killed, and now he is all alone in the world. Imagine how he feels."

Tanner's shoulders slumped after hearing Polina's words. He didn't have to imagine what the wolf was going through. He had lived it. He was the sole survivor of a massacre that ripped his family from his life when he was not much older than Polina.

Sara reached out and caressed Tanner's cheek. She knew something of his past, and understood what he must be feeling.

"Lone wolves can find new pack mates. They don't need to be alone their whole lives."

Tanner looked at her, and as he did so, he felt something stir in his heart. Although they'd only been a couple for a few weeks, their history spanned far more time than that, along with a wide spectrum of emotions, beginning at hate, and ending at… love?

"Thank you, Sara."

"For what?"

"For giving a damn."

"I give more than a damn, you know?"

"I know… and so do I."

"What are you two talking about?" Polina said.

Tanner remembered the scarf he found in Volya's pocket. He took it out and wrapped it around Polina's graceful neck, for extra warmth.

"Sara and I were discussing something personal, and it's time to move out."

Polina smiled as she touched the scarf. "My neck was cold. Thank you, Tanner."

"You're welcome," Tanner said, but he was looking over at the tracks they'd made earlier, which were only faint depressions. A few more minutes of heavy snow and they'd fill in completely.

They headed east with Tanner in the lead and Polina and Sara moving along with care. They were the hunted, and the deadliest of prey.

15
MUSH!

When they were reaching the top of the ridge, Tanner raised a hand, indicating that Sara and Polina should stop walking. They did so, and heard the faint whine of a snowmobile's engine.

"That's Pavel maneuvering behind us, while Matthews and the others head toward us," Tanner said.

"We will outsmart them and take the snowmobile," Polina said. "But Tanner, what if Pavel has the key?"

"I'll figure out a way to start it, but on most older models you just have to lift the hood, reach in, and yank out the ignition switch to open the circuit."

"It's that easy?" Sara said.

"It can be."

The whine of the snowmobile ended, and Tanner came across the tracks the machine had made when it passed by. Something about the angle of the snow caught Tanner's attention. It looked too flat. After taking out a knife, Tanner dug at the snow and found what appeared to be an old concrete road surface. There were wide cracks all through the section he could see, but it was a welcome sight.

"At some point in the past, this area was more populated. There's a road under the snow."

Sara greeted the news with a nod, while grimacing in pain. Her knee had paid a price for making the climb, and her limp was becoming a hobble. Polina helped her to move along, but Tanner saw no reason to wear Sara out. He guided them both behind a fallen pine tree that still had green needles showing.

"Rest here. Once I get the snowmobile I'll come back and get you, since we'll be heading north anyway."

Sara looked relieved. "I could use the rest. My knee is bad, Tanner. I think I'll need to see a doctor when we get back."

Tanner kissed her, then placed a finger playfully on the tip of Polina's nose.

"Stay alert for any sounds. And don't forget, there's a big bad wolf roaming about."

Sara smiled. "That could describe you."

Tanner smiled back at her, and moments later, he was lost in the swirl of white coming down.

MILES AWAY, JACQUES DURAND WAS LOOKING AT THE REAR ends of two Siberian huskies as he rode along in Sasha's sled. The sled dogs were about the only thing he could see as the thick snow came down on an incoming angle.

Sasha told him that they were doing only nine miles an hour because of poor visibility, but it felt faster than that. With the effect the snow made, Durand had the constant feeling of flying down a white tunnel.

They'd been out since dawn, and he was growing

disheartened by the vastness of the landscape and the lack of anything man-made. He was also freezing, despite having put on four layers of clothing and a thick pair of mittens.

Sasha took his advice and headed south. She informed Durand that there weren't any clearings or fields in that direction long enough to land a plane on. However, there was good news. If the small plane Tanner and Sara had been riding in developed trouble, there were three lakes large enough to use as landing strips. Sasha headed to the lake farthest south first and, if there was time, they could check the others as they headed back.

Durand spotted the tail of Yaromir's plane, but before he could point it out to Sasha, he felt the dogs change direction and head toward the plane wreck. If they hadn't been ground level, the plane would have gone unnoticed, as inches of snow coated the wreck. Just a spot of red lettering peeked out of the snow coating the aircraft's tail section, but it had been enough to stand out.

"That looks bad," Durand said, but when he looked up at her, he saw that Sasha was smiling.

"Oh, I've seen much worse. I think someone must have walked away from this."

Her opinion changed as they drew closer, and it became evident that the small plane had been shot to pieces.

Sasha gave Durand a guarded look. "Is there something you forgot to tell me?"

Durand dug into an inner pocket and brought out his official ID and badge. "You're a cop?"

"Of a sort, and my friends work with me. I think they were chased here by someone wanting to kill them."

Sasha kicked at the snow and uncovered several brass casings. "Do you want me to check the plane for you?"

Durand grimaced at the thought of what he might discover inside the plane, but he was not a man who shied away from the truth or avoided unpleasant tasks. "I'll do it," he said.

"All right, but be careful, she's sitting near a hole in the ice, and it looks like it made another one back that way when it first hit."

"How thick is the ice here?"

"As cold as it's been? This ice is plenty thick, but if you feel the plane moving, jump free of it. You're better off breaking an ankle than you'd be falling in that icy water fully clothed."

Durand took off the mittens so he could climb easier, and his fingers stung from the cold wind blowing across the lake. He clambered onto the wing, which was on a precarious angle and coated with frost. Durand steadied himself by grabbing hold of an antenna.

When he cleared away the snow from the door and saw that someone had used duct tape to seal it shut, it perplexed him. And when he realized what it meant, he steeled himself for the worst. Someone had sealed the cabin so that no animals could disturb the contents, namely, a corpse. That meant someone had died.

The plane shuddered and dipped lower. Durand slipped, but managed to keep his grip on the antenna.

Sasha asked Durand to get off the plane, as she feared for him, but he ignored her and ripped open the door. He found the old man, Yaromir. Someone had given him the dignity of covering him with a shirt.

Duran smiled. Sara was alive.

"Poor old man," Sasha said. She had come up behind Durand and her head was at the height of his waist, which meant the plane had dipped a foot deeper into the water.

"He must have died on impact. The bullet wounds bled little," Durand said.

"So your friends survived, that's great. But how did they walk away from all this firepower?"

"Sara Blake is resourceful, and Tanner, well… he is not a man known for losing, regardless of the odds."

"What are they, like secret agents?"

Durand ignored the question and pointed north. "We should have passed them on the way here."

"We may have in this storm, but it's a wide area. They may have heard the dogs, but we'd never hear them call to us with this harsh wind."

Durand looked back the way they'd come and saw that their tracks were filling in. At the rate the snow was coming down, two feet of accumulation sounded like an underestimation.

Sasha laid a hand on his arm. "We can't do much more out here, Mr. Durand, not in this storm. But here's what I'll do, on our return trip, I'll go slower and weave back and forth. If your friends are out there, we should come across their tracks."

"That sounds good, yes, let's do that."

Sasha tossed a GPS tracker inside the plane. She had duct tape, and Durand used a fresh strip to seal the cabin door again.

Back north they went, while weaving east to west, and the snow kept falling and falling.

16

PEEPING TOM

Tanner found the snowmobile and went to work getting it started. The key was gone, but that was to be expected. What Tanner hadn't foreseen, was that Pavel had taken out the spark plugs. That was only an inconvenience. Tanner could retrieve the plugs from Pavel's corpse once he killed the man.

The snowmobile had an electronic gas gauge which was useless with the engine off. But after using a stick to check the fuel level, Tanner saw that there was barely any gas left in the tank. It was certainly not enough to get them back to the city, but it was a sufficient amount to aid Pavel in hunting them down.

Tanner's first impulse was to ruin the machine so that no one could use it, but then, a better idea occurred to him. After damaging the steering stem, Tanner took a rag he'd found beneath the snowmobile's seat, dipped an end of it in the tank, and smeared gasoline in strategic places beneath the hood.

It was a crude booby-trap, but if it worked, Pavel might

break his neck, or be badly burned. In any event, he would be on foot like the rest of them.

Pavel's boot prints, although fading, were still visible. Tanner followed, but stopped every now and then to listen and make sure that Pavel hadn't doubled back.

When the shooting began, Tanner moved behind a tree for cover, but no shots came his way. The sound of raised voices did carry to him, the voices of Gleb and his brother, Aleksandr. They had been firing at the wolf again, and once more they had missed it.

It was remarkable for a pack of wolves to attack a single human. The lone wolf hunting Matthews' party must be mad to risk attacking a group of armed people. Tanner wondered if the beast could be rabid.

A third voice shouted. It was Pavel and he was furious. Tanner moved closer to be able to see what was going on, and to do that, he took to the trees. When he reached a height of twenty feet, he could see them. Given the swirling snow, they were indistinct, but their voices carried on the wind.

Being up in the tree had sparked a memory, and Tanner recalled another time and another tree, and of the man who had been stalking Genevieve on that long ago hunting trip.

CODY AND HIS GRANDFATHER HAD WOKEN EARLY AND GONE out to the parking lot to start the old man's truck and let it run for a while. It had been a frigid night with the temperature dipping into the single digits. Cody's grandfather wanted to be sure his pickup truck would start.

They hadn't needed to use the truck since they arrived for

the hunting trip, but the engine kicked over right away, and the battery seemed strong. With the truck running and time to kill, they went for a drive about the area. There wasn't much to see, and other than the ranch, there were only a few homes spaced about, most of which were smaller ranches.

A trip into the nearby community revealed that only the coffee shop was open at such an early hour, so they decided to eat in town and skip the morning meal at the lodge.

"You'll be eating alone tonight, Cody. I'll be having dinner with Genevieve's mom, Deanna, in the lodge's dining room."

"Oh, okay, but can I order room service?"

"Yes sir, and have anything you want."

"Genevieve will be eating alone too, maybe she'll let me hang out with her."

"Is she talking to you yet?"

"She was just grossed out by watching me field dress the deer. She'll get over it. She likes me."

Cody's grandfather smiled. "You're a confident one. Hold on to that. Boldness is a rare quality in this world."

THEY RETURNED TO THE LODGE, AND AS THEY WERE walking back from the parking lot, Cody spotted the man up in the tree. The tree was across from a snow-covered hill that faced the rear of some of the rooms. One of those rooms belonged to Genevieve and her mother. The man hiding among the branches was looking down into it while peering from binoculars.

"Grandddad, look at that guy in the tree. I think he's a peeping Tom."

Walter Parker squinted, but couldn't make out the man's face, or even his age.

"Hey! Buddy, what are you doing up in that tree?"

The man in the tree startled after hearing the old man's shouted words. He dropped the binoculars into the snow and nearly lost his footing upon the branch he stood on. As Cody and his grandfather moved closer, the man half-climbed, half-jumped off the tree and ran into the forest.

Cody's grandfather shook his head in disgust. "Damn weirdo. I'll let the lodge know they have a peeper in the area."

The man was more than a peeping Tom. Hours later, he'd return to the lodge and abduct Genevieve.

17

PAY ATTENTION

From his vantage point up in the tree, Tanner watched Pavel as he marched toward Gleb and Aleksandr. It struck Tanner that Pavel had the bearing and demeanor of someone who had served in the military.

Gleb and Aleksandr were much taller than Pavel and twice his weight each, but Pavel showed no fear of their greater size as he berated the brothers for firing at the wolf.

"Did you not understand that we were trying to place Tanner in a pincer movement, and that it required stealth?"

"Yeah, but Pavel, we can't let that wolf live. He killed Volya," Gleb said.

"And how many has Tanner killed? I saw your planes, your other men, we need to kill Tanner and I need to get the girl back. If you're too stupid to see that, I suggest you separate from us."

Aleksandr stepped closer to Pavel. If it was an attempt to intimidate the man, Aleksandr had failed. Pavel didn't even blink, not even when Gleb moved beside his brother, the two behemoths forming a wall of flesh.

Gleb pushed Pavel by shoving the smaller man in the chest. "Call us stupid again and we'll hurt you."

Pavel turned his head and spoke to the others. "Pay attention. This will be a good lesson for you to learn."

A knife appeared in Pavel's hand as if by magic. That same hand moved in a blur, then Pavel pushed between Gleb and Aleksandr until he was standing behind them.

An instant later, the brothers' necks gushed blood and sent streams of red into the snow. Gleb grabbed onto Aleksandr as Aleksandr took hold of him. Each man had been hoping the other would help him, only to discover that they'd both been dealt the same fate.

The brothers reached out to stem the flow of blood on each other's neck in a futile attempt to stave off death. While Liliya vomited at the sight of the spurting blood, Gleb and Aleksandr fell first to their knees, then settled on their sides, where they died while facing each other.

After dipping the blade in the snow, Pavel wiped it clean on Gleb's pant leg and put it away. He then pointed his rifle at the others. They all took a step backwards.

"If you can't help me kill Tanner and retrieve the girl, then I have no use for you. Spread out, look for tracks, and find that bastard."

Fedor took Liliya's hand and moved away. "I'll find Tanner, Pavel, and I'll kill him."

"Good man, but do not harm the girl."

Nikolai and Boz went off together, while Matthews chose a different direction, after taking a final look at Gleb and Aleksandr's bodies.

∼

Up in the tree, Tanner had seen Pavel kill the two brothers. The man had been as graceful as a swan as he moved, graceful, deadly, and experienced.

Tanner didn't know about the others, but Dan Matthews was smart enough to figure out that, no matter the outcome, Pavel would kill them all. Matthews was headed north into the storm and away from Pavel. If the others had any sense, they'd be doing likewise.

After climbing down from the tree, Tanner headed back toward the area where he'd left Sara and Polina. Were he alone and working under normal conditions, Tanner would kill them all, starting with the fleeing Matthews. But he had a woman with an injured knee and a kidnapped child to think about.

There was also the storm, which was fierce and dropping snow at a quickening pace. They had to find a place of shelter, or else create one, and they had to do it soon.

Nikolai, Fedor, and the woman, Liliya, were concerns, but minor ones. The true threats were the weather and Pavel.

While it would be nice if the booby-trapped snowmobile would finish the man off, Tanner doubted that outcome.

He would rejoin Sara and Polina, shelter them from the storm, and then find Pavel and kill him. Tanner only hoped the man would have the grace to die easily. However, he didn't think it would end that way.

18

NOT EXACTLY WHAT I'D CALL FIRST AID

When Tanner returned to them, he saw that Sara had fashioned a crude cane out of a tree branch to help her walk. He also noticed the worried look in Polina's eyes and asked her what was wrong.

Polina hugged herself. "I miss the pit. At least it was warm and kept us out of the snow."

"We'll be warm again soon, but the snowmobile isn't an option. Pavel made sure only he could use it and there wasn't much fuel left either."

"Did you disable it?" Sara asked.

"I went one better and sabotaged it. But enough talk, we need to find a place to hunker down."

"What does 'hunker down' mean?" Polina asked.

Tanner brushed frost off her shoulders. "It means we'll be warm and out of the snow."

They continued walking along the ridge and the signs that it had once been a narrow road increased, as sections of concrete curbing stuck up out of the snow here and there. When what looked like a fallen tree turned out to be an old wooden light pole, Tanner tried his phone again, but had no signal.

Then, the buildings appeared, looking like wooden lumps. They were old and rotted and the wind blew snow into them from large gaps in their sagging roofs.

Faded paint showed that they had been built and used by the military of the former Soviet Union. Given their state of decay, they were no good as shelter, but their wood could be used to feed a fire.

Tanner found dry wood lying beneath debris, and several of the larger boards would serve as snow scoops or shovels. Tanner ripped them free and carried them along.

Sara was making a soft grunt of pain with each step she took by the time Tanner found the right place to settle. It was a natural lump of earth, or perhaps someone in years past had dumped dirt on the spot, but it made for a handy windbreak. It was near enough to the buildings to see them in good weather. However, when he looked back at the structures, Tanner saw that they were little more than dark shapes behind a relentless wall of falling snow.

"Why settle here and not back at the buildings?" Sara asked. "There was still one wall there that was under a good section of roof."

"I don't know who might come along, but they'll surely be drawn to those ruins."

"Yes, but we need shelter."

"Once I build our quinzee, we'll have shelter, and we'll blend in to our surroundings."

Beneath the fur cap she wore, Sara wrinkled her brow. "What's a quinzee?"

"It's like an igloo. The first thing I'll do is tramp down the snow here. Afterwards, we gather together a large pile of snow. Polina, that will be your job. You can use one of the boards like a shovel."

Polina beamed. "I made a quinzee before with the Girl Scouts, but this one must be bigger."

"Yes, but there's more, we need to build for defense too."

Tanner described what they were going to do. Sara agreed it was a good plan, but said she felt useless with her bad knee.

Tanner explained her role as he and Polina stamped down the snow where they would build the quinzee. "Sara, you'll be keeping guard. I can't build this and watch my back at the same time."

"That's true, isn't it?" Sara said. She was already doing her part, as she held a rifle at the ready. "All right, but I'd feel better about this if we knew where Matthews, Pavel, and the others were."

"I'll hunt down Pavel once you two have shelter, as for the others, the storm will kill them. They have no food, heat, or common sense."

"Why go after Pavel, is he that much of a threat?"

"Yeah Sara, that man is the real deal. By the way he carries himself, I'd say he's former military, and he's good. I won't sleep until I know he's been handled."

"What about the booby-trap you set?"

Tanner smiled as he helped Polina pile up snow where the ground was trampled.

"My guess is Pavel has discovered my trick by now."

TANNER WAS RIGHT. AT THAT VERY MOMENT, PAVEL WAS lying on his back in the snow. He had replaced the spark plugs, started the snowmobile, and sped away to look for Tanner, Sara, and Polina.

When he reached the first spot where he needed to

turn, the snowmobile refused to go in the new direction. Pavel tried to stop, but a tree made that possible before he could. He flew off the seat, turned over in midair, and bounced hard off a second tree, after slamming into it with his hip.

Pavel stood, as he grimaced in pain. After that impact, he knew he'd soon have one hell of a bruise on his hip. He reminded himself not to underestimate Tanner. The assassin had found his snowmobile, and unable to use it for himself, he used it against Pavel.

Pavel looked back at the machine and saw that a fire had begun in the engine. No doubt, it was more of Tanner's doing. A stoic man by nature, Pavel took it all in stride, that is, until he saw the pieces of his satellite phone lying in his tracks. Pavel reached under his jacket and took the phone off his hip. It had taken the brunt of the impact when he had hit the tree. The unit was useless. A barrage of curses followed that discovery, but they were cut short.

The woman, Liliya, was screaming, and from the sound of it she was in great pain. Pavel moved in the direction of the disturbance with haste, but also a sense of caution. There was always the chance that Tanner was torturing Liliya to draw the others in.

Whatever the case may be, Pavel had to know what was behind it, but he could offer a guess before he even reached her. Paw prints were in the snow, paw prints such as a wolf would make, and they were bloody and fresh.

FEDOR HAD SPOTTED THE WOLF FIRST, AS HE AND LILIYA walked along in the storm looking for any sign of Tanner. The beast was charging at them, at him! Aware that he'd never bring his rifle to bear in time, Fedor shoved Liliya toward the wolf, and the two of them collided.

Liliya still had no idea what was going on. She landed on the snow sitting up, heard a growl, and turned her head. When she saw the wolf's fangs, saw the glittering eyes, smelled the stench of its hot breath, she screamed.

That made the wolf stop growling. The apex predator might have considered Liliya unworthy prey, but frightened and filled with a sense of panic, Liliya began striking the wolf on its snout. She connected three times. On her fourth attempt, the wolf swallowed her hand, bit down, and broke her wrist.

While this was going on, Fedor stood frozen, rifle in hand. He was afraid to move, too fearful to so much as breathe, lest the wolf pounce on him.

Liliya used her free hand to pummel the wolf in the face, but the wolf shook his head and she was knocked onto her side. Liliya kicked and screamed. The wolf released her hand and bit her face, ripping away the flesh that had been her right cheek.

The scream that followed was monumental. Her cheek wound was followed by two fingers on her right hand being bitten off at the second knuckle. Then, more bites to the face, including one that blinded her left eye, while her nose was ripped away.

Liliya's neck, while cut by the wolf's fangs, remained intact thanks to a turtleneck sweater and a scarf.

Liliya's kicking legs were bitten on the calf, but as shouts of concern rose in the distance from Nikolai and Boz, the wolf retreated, leaving behind a disfigured woman and a coward of a man.

Pavel arrived first and saw that Fedor had done nothing to help. Fedor was still frozen in place. He was looking down at the screaming, thrashing Liliya as tears spilled from his eyes.

Then came Nikolai. He was running so fast that he slipped and fell while still yards away. When he looked up and saw what had befallen Liliya, he crawled through the snow to get to her. Nikolai tried to hold her, to soothe her, but the agony of Liliya's wounds made her writhe out of his grip.

Boz crossed himself, then, he became furious. After slinging his rifle over his back, he took hold of Fedor and shook him.

Although Boz's rage was directed at Fedor, it was fueled by his own feelings of guilt. He had failed to fire at the wolf as it attacked Volya, and instead, had run away in fright. Seeing Fedor standing there frozen in inaction had reminded him of his own lack of courage.

"Why didn't you shoot, Fedor? You must have had a shot!"

Fedor's crying turned into sobs, and he sank to the ground. Then, Fedor was on his back, as Nikolai strangled the life out of him.

Pavel shook his head at the madness before him.

Nature, which included both wolf and storm, was trying its best to kill them, but these poor specimens he'd been forced to join forces with were killing each other. Be it through cowardice or rage, they would lose two more people, while Tanner made away with Polina.

Fedor fought feebly, perhaps a coward accepting his fate, or rage and indignation empowering Nikolai.

Whatever forces were at play, when Nikolai rose from

the ground, Fedor was dead. Nikolai's face was bloodied from a split lip, but it was his only injury.

Nikolai pointed down at Liliya. Her screaming had ceased, to be replaced by the murmur of wretched moaning, and she had rolled into the fetal position.

Nikolai grabbed Pavel's right arm. "We have to get Liliya to a hospital. You have a snowmobile. I know you do. I heard the sound of it coming from up on the ridge. Where is it?"

"Tanner destroyed it. It is useless."

"No! Why would he do that?"

"To even the odds, but I will kill him anyway."

Nikolai paced in a circle for a moment, before positioning himself behind Liliya.

"Boz, help me. You take her legs while I pick her up. We'll carry her. We'll carry her all the way back to the city if we have—"

The gunshot was loud, but somehow muffled, as it reverberated off the ubiquitous falling snow. It was a single shot from Pavel's Makarov pistol, and it had blown the top of Liliya's head off.

Nikolai stared down at the dead body of the only woman he had ever loved, and sanity fled from his mind. "Liliya? Baby, get up, oh please get up."

Pavel raised the gun and took aim at Nikolai's chest. As he was about to pull the trigger, Boz rushed at him from the opposite side. Pavel readjusted and fired across his body. A round caught Boz in the forehead, the tall biker's momentum kept him coming even though he was dead, and he fell heavily against Pavel.

Pavel was not a large man, but he was strong. He kept his balance, but then saw Nikolai taking aim with a rifle. As Pavel stepped back to let Boz slide to the snow, he and Nikolai fired at each other.

Nikolai's shot missed, Pavel's did not, and Nikolai fell to the ground, still alive, but wounded and unconscious. Nikolai's bloody scalp touched Liliya's, as her brain acted as his pillow.

Believing he had killed Nikolai, Pavel turned his attention away from him and claimed Fedor's rifle. He checked the weapon, saw that it was fully loaded, and removed the useful ammo from it. Afterward, he headed off to track down Tanner.

It had not escaped his notice that Matthews had never appeared on the scene.

Pavel sighed. Someone else to kill.

And the snow kept right on falling.

19

WEEPING AND GNASHING OF TEETH

Polina was turning out to be a gem.

The teen worked with determined energy and a good spirit. In less time than he'd imagined it taking, Tanner's modified quinzee was almost ready.

"We still have to dig out the vent hole for the fire, Tanner," Polina said.

"A fire? Won't it melt?" Sara asked.

"Not if we vent properly," Tanner said. "And the space inside won't be hot, but it will be above freezing. We'll also be able to heat the food in the MRE's. Before we settle in, I'll gather more wood from the ruins."

Sara was standing watch while Tanner and Polina worked. Whenever she spoke, her eyes were busy looking around for movement, as well as color. With the world turning white, any color stood out in stark contrast.

"Are you still going to look for Pavel?"

"I have to, Sara. He's too dangerous to leave roaming about."

"I wish my knee wasn't injured. I could back you up."

"Polina needs you anyway. I wouldn't leave her alone."

"I would be all right, Tanner. I have my knife now," Polina said.

"Yeah, and the guts to use it, I'm sure."

Tanner and Polina finished the quinzee by placing a blanket atop the packed snow that was its floor. Then, Polina assisted Sara, as she crawled inside it without trying to place weight on her bad knee.

The space was large enough to sit up inside, but not big enough to stand in. Within the fireplace at the rear, Tanner started a blaze by using one of the dry fuel tablets from a Russian MRE. In a short time, the quinzee felt warm, and Sara and Polina removed their fur hats. Tanner kept his knit cap on, as he was going back out.

"I'll go to those old buildings and get more wood. I also need to find something that will give us a flap for a door. That way, we'll keep the heat inside."

"We'll start warming the food," Sara said. "Then we'll eat when you come back."

Tanner had been gone for several minutes when Polina scurried out the opening.

"I'll help Tanner gather wood."

Sara called for her to come back, but the girl kept going. Sara smiled. Polina had a crush on Tanner and must have wanted to spend time with him alone. In a way, her infatuation was a blessing. It kept the girl's mind off her situation and the sadness of being separated from her family.

To Sara's surprise, the snow shelter was comfortable, and the warmth, although minor, felt delicious. She'd been leaning with her back against a wall, while on the verge of falling asleep, but Sara sat bolt upright with eyes wide open after hearing Polina scream.

WHITE HELL

AFTER LEAVING SARA AND POLINA INSIDE THE QUINZEE, Tanner had rushed off to get more wood. The snow was coming down with such density that he was mere yards away from the buildings before he could distinguish them from the enveloping wall of white.

A piece of dry canvas found under a collapsed wall would make a great cover for the snow shelter's doorway. The cloth was an off-white color, and would be good camouflage as well.

Tanner stuffed the canvas under his jacket and filled his arms with wood before heading back toward the snow shelter.

He was halfway there when he saw the first paw prints and knew that the wolf was in the area. When he studied the paw prints and followed their path, Tanner saw that they led into the trees. A few steps later, he saw new paw prints. They looked fresh, as if the wolf had just made them. While looking to see where they led, Tanner became aware of movement on his left. When he turned that way, he saw Pavel smiling at him while aiming a rifle his way.

"That wood looks burdensome, and I take it you're Tanner."

"Look closely at the wood, Pavel."

The smile left Pavel's face when he saw the tip of a gun barrel sticking out from the wood.

"I guess we have a standoff," Pavel said. "Although, I could risk shooting you anyway."

"And I could shoot back and wound you, which, given the conditions out here, is as good as killing you."

"A wound in this weather is a death sentence," Pavel agreed. "But I have an idea."

"I thought you might," Tanner said, while knowing what the man was thinking.

Recalling what he'd learned from Polina, Tanner knew

that Pavel was deadly with his hands. The man was confident of coming out on top in any unarmed combat.

Pavel took one hand off the rifle, held it up in a gesture of peace, then slowly lowered his weapon and sat it on the snow.

"You could shoot me now, Tanner, but if I have a breath left, I'll claim the rifle and shoot you back. Or, you could be man enough to fight me."

Tanner nearly squeezed the trigger on his gun, but the whirlwind of white filling the air made visibility a problem. He was not certain he could kill Pavel with one shot, and given the man's abilities, Pavel might reclaim his rifle and fire back.

As Pavel said, a wound would be fatal. If you didn't bleed to death, the cold would kill you. Tanner let the firewood fall, dropped the gun, and took a step forward.

Pavel was a dangerous opponent with his expertise in Combat Sambo. Tanner could tell within the first few seconds of their contest that Pavel was a disciplined fighter. Pavel's leg sweep was the fastest Tanner had ever seen, but he'd been expecting it.

Pavel took Tanner's legs out from under him and grabbed his right wrist, while shoving him downward.

Tanner fell on his back while fighting the natural urge to use his free hand to cushion the fall. Then, before Pavel could follow through with a blow to his face or neck, Tanner smashed a fist against the man's testicles.

Pavel reacted by releasing Tanner and rolling backwards. The pain and nausea Tanner had inflicted were displayed on Pavel's face, along with something else. It was a look of annoyance. Tanner wasn't playing by the rules and Pavel looked offended by such an obvious breach of combat etiquette.

Tanner had no doubt that Pavel could beat him nine

times out of ten in a regulated match with rules. But there were no rules in Tanner's world, save for one, kill or be killed. No one was better at that game. No one.

Both men had risen to their feet when Polina appeared. She stared at Pavel with horror, although Pavel greeted her appearance with a smile.

"Hello Polina. I've come to get you."

"Polina," Tanner said. "Go back to Sara and tell her to stay there until I return."

Polina nodded, but stood frozen, as Pavel moved toward Tanner.

Pavel threw a punch that Tanner blocked easily. It had been a set up for an attempted hip throw. However, as Pavel turned around to begin the toss, Tanner bit the back of his neck.

So shocked was Pavel by the unexpected act, that he flubbed the hip toss, and he and Tanner fell on the snow in a jumble of arms and legs. Pavel rolled away once more, felt the back of his neck and came away with a bloody hand.

"You fight like a woman, Tanner."

"What's the matter? I'm not following the rules."

"There are ways around that. I look forward to killing you."

As Polina watched, Pavel charged at Tanner and sent a flying kick at his head. Tanner avoided it, but had felt a feather touch of contact against his left ear.

Pavel then connected with a side kick that made Tanner huff out a breath. It was followed by another side kick, then another. Tanner was being driven back while attempting to draw in a breath. Pavel's feet moved like lightning and the snow didn't affect his balance at all.

After delivering a backhand blow that stunned Pavel, Tanner had time to recover. But he hurt on the left side. If not for the layers of clothing he wore, he thought Pavel might have cracked a rib. The smaller man was strong, and as quick as anyone Tanner had ever faced.

Tanner blocked Pavel's next kick and felt his arm go numb. When he blocked the following kick, which struck his left elbow, the numbness went away. It had been replaced by a sharp pain, pain so deep and sudden that Tanner cried out and backed away.

When he looked down, Tanner saw that his arm was sitting crooked. Pavel had dislocated his elbow, or perhaps broken his arm.

When Polina noticed the odd angle of Tanner's arm, she screamed.

"Polina go! Now!" Tanner shouted.

The teen ignored him, took out her knife, and advanced on Pavel while crying. Pavel flicked out a foot and sent the knife hurling into the air. When it landed near a tree, Polina spun and ran back toward the snow shelter.

"I'll get Sara!"

Tanner shouted to her. "Damn it no! Polina!"

Pavel smiled. "Don't concern yourself over the girl or your woman. You'll be dead before they return."

Pavel, full of confidence, charged at Tanner and took him down with a scissor throw by wrapping his legs around Tanner's middle. As Pavel reared back a fist, Tanner spat in his eye. Pavel jerked his head and the blow aimed at Tanner's face missed.

Pavel reddened with rage as he wiped the spittle from his face. Tanner laughed at him as he moved away, which made Pavel furious.

The Russian charged in, landed a glancing blow on Tanner's bad arm, then attempted the hip throw again. It succeeded, and Pavel had Tanner flat on his back, as he lay across Tanner's chest. It proved to be Pavel's undoing.

Tanner stretched his neck and brought his head up as high as he could, opened his mouth, and clamped down hard on the flesh of Pavel's throat. Pavel let out a scream, released Tanner, and this time when he rolled away, he left a vital piece of flesh behind.

Tanner's mouth was bloody, and he spat out the hunk of skin he'd ripped from Pavel's throat.

Pavel sat up on his knees, looked at the hand he'd pressed against his neck and saw that it was dripping blood.

After washing his mouth out with snow, Tanner got to his feet and walked over to stare down at Pavel.

"A wound *can* kill you in this weather, and it doesn't take a gun."

Pavel stood, fell, stood again, then sat in the snow. Blood poured from his wound and Tanner surmised that he had nicked the man's carotid artery. When Pavel lunged toward his rifle, Tanner walked over and picked it up, then kicked Pavel in the face.

Pavel stared up at him as he gasped in the cold air. He said nothing else, but wore a look of incrimination as he shook his head.

Tanner understood. The man was telling him that he had fought an unfair fight and won without honor. Tanner didn't give a damn about rules and never had. It was part of what made him who he was and one of the reasons he was still alive.

Pavel died an instant before Sara appeared. She was hobbling along on her makeshift cane and holding a gun up with one hand, following far behind her was Polina, with a face full of tears.

Tanner helped Sara to stand. By rushing out to aid him, she had only made her knee worse.

"The blood, oh, and look at your arm," she said.

"I think my elbow's dislocated, and the blood is Pavel's. He's dead."

Polina hugged Tanner, then went over to stare down at Pavel. "Damn you for killing Stas," she said in Russian, then kicked the body. Before leaving the area, she plucked her knife from where it had fallen in the snow.

Sara's cane was not enough, and she was having difficulty in the deepening snow. Tanner picked her up with his one good arm and carried her back to the quinzee, as Polina gathered some of the wood and followed.

Once inside the shelter, Sara checked Tanner's pulse near his wrist. She was worried that his injury may have cut off the flow of blood to his lower arm, but all seemed well.

Tanner instructed Polina on how to put up the tarp over the shelter's opening, then the three of them huddled together with Polina in the middle and ate from an MRE.

Polina was on Tanner's right, while his left arm was in a makeshift sling that Sara had made for him. Once they'd eaten, they listened to the wind howl as the sun set.

"Tanner, what are we going to do?" Polina asked.

"We're going to hunker down," Tanner said. "And tomorrow we'll make it back to the city."

Polina squeezed under Tanner's good arm and lay her head on his chest.

"I like this hunker down, but I miss my family."

"You'll see them soon," Sara said.

Polina smiled at her, yawned, and fell asleep.

"Do you want the first watch, or should I take it," Sara asked.

"Wake me in four hours," Tanner said. "And keep feeding that fire."

"Hey."

"Yeah?"

Sara stared over at him. Tanner had to be feeling the pain from his arm injury, but he dealt with it in his usual imperturbable manner. Still, he looked as tired as she'd ever seen him, and he held Polina safe and secure under one arm.

"My knee is shot. I don't think I could walk even a mile in deep snow, and you have only one good arm."

"We'll deal with it, don't worry."

Sara smiled. "Do you ever worry about anything?"

"Not often."

"Get some sleep."

Tanner nodded, closed his eyes, and was asleep within minutes.

Sara sat there, watching him, as thoughts and feelings engulfed her. Tanner was unlike anyone she'd ever known. Sara watched her man sleep, as she thought about her growing love for him.

"He is Tanner," Polina had said.

Sara smiled. He sure as hell was.

20

GOOD FOR THE SOUL

Jacques Durand was disheartened that his search for Sara was taking so long, and he wondered if she and Tanner were still battling more than bad weather.

Durand was colder than he'd ever been by the time he and Sasha returned to the city. When Sasha asked him where he was staying, Durand shivered and said he didn't know.

"My luggage is sitting out there in my rental car. I started looking for a search plane before I thought of getting a hotel."

"The latest weather forecast says this storm is a monster, but that it will burn itself out by dawn. Do you still want to get an early start?"

"Oh yes, a good meal and a few hours of sleep and I'll be ready to go again."

"Stay here then, if you don't mind sleeping on a couch. My niece made venison stew and biscuits, we have a fireplace, and with this storm, the streets will be hard to travel."

Durand nodded in agreement. He had not been

looking forward to being alone all evening, while worry nibbled at his mind. "Thank you, Sasha, I accept, and I'll pay you extra for it."

"No, you will not. This is an act of friendship."

"You're very kind."

The niece's name was Brenda. Brenda was visiting from San Francisco, but also spent her summers with Sasha and her husband. Sasha's husband was named Brett, and the storm had delayed his return home.

With a tasty stew and strong black tea fortifying him, Durand was feeling warm again. Along with knowing how to cook, Brenda was also an amateur mechanic. She had fixed a broken snowmobile while they'd been out searching. She said she would help search for Sara and Tanner the next day. Durand made another new friend when he paid Brenda for helping.

"Thanks, I would have done it for free, Mr. Durand, but I can use the money too."

"You're welcome, and both of you, please call me Jacques."

Brenda went to her room to video chat with a friend back home and Sasha poured vodka for herself and Durand.

With the layers of outerwear stripped away, Duran saw that Sasha had a good figure to go with her pretty face and long raven hair. The picture of her and her husband sitting on the mantle showed a handsome man with dark-blond hair and sparkling blue eyes. Durand thought if Sasha ever had children that they would be beautiful.

Once they were on their second drinks, Sasha asked Durand about Sara.

"Are you two close?"

"Not really, but I care for her."

"Is it mutual?"

"We are friends."

"Oh, I thought that maybe something more was going on there… you seem quite fond of her."

Durand finished his second vodka and looked down into his empty glass. "I'm smitten by Sara, like a damn schoolboy. I know it's ridiculous, but it's how I feel."

"Are you seeing anyone."

"Not since my wife died."

Sasha poured more vodka into Durand's glass. "I'm sorry you lost someone, Jacques. Was it recent?"

"No, it's been years, long years."

"This Sara, does she know that you have feelings for her?"

"Perhaps, but I'm nearly twice her age and she already has someone. These feelings I have for her will lead to nothing. Maybe I'm just getting old and missing my youth."

"You're not that old, Jacques, and falling for someone has nothing to do with age. I had the terrible hots for a married man once. Nothing happened between us, but I just knew I'd never want anyone else. Then I met my husband. When this is over and you're back home, go on a date with someone, several women even. Maybe you're just lonely."

Durand smiled at Sasha. "You are a wise woman."

Sasha stood with the bottle in her hand. "I'm wise enough to know I've had enough vodka if I'm getting on a sled at first light. Use the hallway bathroom, it's got a shower, and there are blankets and pillows in the closet over there. Goodnight, Jacques."

"Goodnight, Sasha, and thank you for everything."

Sasha smiled from the foot of the stairs. "Sometimes it helps to confess your feelings to someone. Get some sleep. We may have a long day tomorrow."

Durand carried his toiletry kit into the bathroom, shaved, showered, and returned to the living room.

It was a huge couch, and comfortable; however, sleep eluded him at first. When it did arrive, it brought dreams of Sara.

21

WHITEOUT!

Dan Matthews was lost.

The world had gone white, as snow was plastered onto every surface he could see. The ground, sky, and even the damn trees were white. The air was filled with white and he was so coated in snow that he looked like a snowman.

His toes and the tips of several fingers were frostbitten. He was certain of it and was aware that he would die if he didn't find shelter soon. He'd almost stopped at the wrecked buildings he'd seen but figured if he gave it a few more hours he could make it back to civilization.

Less than an hour later, the storm seemed to double in size and he knew he'd made a mistake. Matthews later realized that he had been turned around and lost all sense of direction. At one point, it was so hard to see, that he walked into a tree. He thought he was still headed north, but that was only a guess after the snow came down in clumps.

Matthews kept trying his phone, but he gave up after coming across a cell tower that had suffered damage. One of the nearby pines had fallen and smashed into the metal structure on its way down. The tree's branches were caught up in the steel framework and the tower's antennas were broken.

And so, Matthews headed deeper into the forest. His hope was that he might find an old hunting cabin to take shelter in, or perhaps even an occupied house.

On the plane ride into the area, Fedor mentioned that there were a few people living within the forest. If he could find one of their homes, he'd beg them to let him inside. If that didn't work, he'd use his gun to make them cooperate.

Having barely slept and not eaten for more than a day, he was exhausted and famished. At least he had water when he wanted it, by eating the snow. Matthews recalled hearing that eating snow wasn't good for you, and that it lowered the body's core temperature. Still, as cold as he was, he was still sweating, so, he foolishly assumed that eating the snow was okay. When he felt he couldn't go another step, Matthews leaned back against a tree.

What a clusterfuck! Damn Blake and Tanner, and that nut job Pavel too. And what is the story behind that girl? I don't believe for a second that she's Pavel's daughter, but then, what are Blake and Tanner doing with her? None of this makes any sense and I'm so damn cold that I wish I were back in prison.

Matthews closed his eyes, while thinking he simply needed to rest for a while. Moments later, he slid to the ground after falling asleep and woke with a start. He looked around at the white landscape. The moon, which was hidden behind the clouds, reflected its light off the snow and lent the night a quality of luminescence.

With his back still against the tree, Matthews closed his eyes again. He was starving, and so tired, just bone weary from trudging through the snow. Furthermore, the bitter cold was keen, and as piercing as any blade. He would have frozen to death where he sat, but a scent wafting in the wind saved him. Matthews' eyes flew open as he sniffed the air.

Wood smoke! I smell wood smoke. There's a house out here somewhere, and I bet they have a fireplace. And food! They must have food, and oh, would I kill for a drink.

He spent the better part of an hour tracking down the source of the wood smoke and found it sitting down a hill, inside a clearing.

It was a small home, a shack really, with a wraparound porch that was crumbling in sections. Other than the windows, which were warmed by the fireplace, the home was as white as everything else. The smoke curling out of the red brick chimney was one of the sweetest sights Matthews had ever seen.

He approached the house from the right side and could see a fallow field covered with snow behind the house. There was also a stream somewhere nearby. Matthews could hear the water trickling over ice, but was unable to see it.

A faint glow lit the structure's filthy windows. Matthews walked to the side of the home and looked in past gray and threadbare lace curtains. The home was a hovel. The place looked filthy and disorganized. The small space was crammed with old furniture, stacks of boxes, and piles of yellowing newspapers, but inside there was heat, blessed heat, thanks to the fireplace.

Movement caught his eye. There was an old woman in there, farther back, in what was the kitchen. She was a frail-looking thing, white-haired and wizened. The old woman was leaning over and removing something from a cast-iron oven. When Matthews caught sight of the roasted chicken, he drooled. The saliva froze on his chin before it could drip off.

The old woman placed the chicken on the stove top, then check the contents of two pans that were sitting on the top section. There was not only heat inside the squalid little house, but food. He left the window and moved toward the front door.

As an explanation for what he was doing wandering the forest during a blizzard, he would say that he survived the crash of a small plane, but that the pilot had died on impact.

At the front of the house, piled up in one corner of the porch was firewood. The other end held a porch swing, but the swing looked old, and was hanging by only one chain.

As a precaution, Matthews decided to move his gun from the front pocket of his coat and conceal it. He didn't want to spook the old lady and doubted he would need a gun to gain entry. However, he didn't know whether she was in there alone, or if there was a man inside, perhaps a burly son.

Matthews realized he must look like a bum, with his burnt pants, but who wouldn't take a stranger in from a storm like this one?

He reached inside the jacket pocket and felt nothing. The gun! Where was the damn gun? Matthews was frantic as he checked his other pockets, while looking for his weapon, but it was no use. It was gone.

Then, he understood what had happened. It must have tumbled out of his jacket pocket and into the snow when he slid down the tree and onto his ass. He let out a soft moan that was drowned out by the wind. Even if he retraced his steps by following his prints in the snow, it would be useless. He had walked past countless trees while tracking down the scent of the wood smoke. He'd never find that particular tree again, not even if his life depended upon it.

With a sigh, he let it go. It didn't matter. There was probably just the old woman to deal with. What was important is that he'd found shelter and food. He was safe.

Matthews used his right hand to pound on the door and felt agony. But, that was good he reasoned. It meant the hand still had some feeling in it.

In his mind's eye, Matthews looked ahead. He imagined himself sitting beside a comfy fire, wrapped inside a blanket, and eating a delicious meal of roast chicken, perhaps with a glass of whisky, or more likely, vodka. His daydream ended when the knocking was answered by barking.

So, the old woman had a pet to keep her company. *That's nice*, Matthews thought, and he liked dogs. Matthews had expected the old woman to shush the animal, or to move it away from the door so that they could talk. He did not expect her to simply open the door and let the beast out, which is what happened. The dog hit Matthews in the chest as it snarled at him. It was a German Shepherd mix of some sort, weighed over sixty pounds, and was filled with fury. Matthews almost fell over, but kept his balance as he screamed in fright.

The old lady was smiling, but she had no teeth left in her mouth. She was also holding an ancient shotgun. Before opening the door, she had tossed on a fur coat that was made from the pelts of rabbits, with a matching cap on her head. She cackled away as Matthews struggled with the dog.

Terrified and panicked, Matthews spoke in his native English instead of Russian, as he begged the woman to call the dog off.

The cackling ceased. Although Matthews had no way of knowing it, the old woman despised Westerners. Her father had been an espionage agent in the Cold War world of the 1950's. He left for an assignment one day and never returned. By speaking English, Matthews had risen from the level of an annoying intrusion, to become a despised enemy.

The shotgun was raised, and if Matthews hadn't slipped and fallen backwards, the blast from the gun would have blown part of his head off.

One of the pellets had hit the dog on its hind quarters. The hound yelped and scurried away from Matthews, as if it thought he was the source of its pain. The beast went back inside the house as the old witch fed a fresh shell into her gun.

Matthews reached out, grabbed a log from the pile, and hurled it at the old woman. The log smacked her on the chin, but she held on to the shotgun. Matthews threw another log, then, another. The last log struck the woman between the eyes and the shotgun went off right before she dropped it. The blast tore a hole in the overhanging roof of the porch, as the old woman wobbled back inside the house.

Matthews made it to his feet and grabbed up the shotgun, then, he stepped inside the door. The old woman stumbled around a dusty sofa with blood streaming down her face from a cut. The mad crone looked like she was about to pass out, and when she did lose consciousness, she fell backwards into the fireplace.

Matthews was rushing over to pull her out when she sprang up from the logs. She had used a hand to support herself, and the odor of the burnt flesh was sickening, while her scream was frightening. Other than the hand, the flames had yet to touch her, but the rabbit fur coat was on fire. The old woman was screaming incoherently as she shed the coat. It landed near a wall and set the curtains on fire. Terror cleared the old woman's mind, and she rushed through a doorway that led to the kitchen.

Matthews was horrified by the turn of events. He had been freezing, and now was in danger of burning to death. When the old lady returned, she was holding a bucket full of water, which she tossed onto the curtains.

However, the sofa had caught fire as well, along with the rug and a pile of newspapers. As the old woman rushed back into the kitchen for more water, embers from the burning newspapers spread throughout the room. Matthews backed out of the house when he saw that fighting the blaze would be useless. The embers had ignited countless small fires and the home was filling with smoke.

There was a tree stump nearby. Matthews cleared off the snow and sat down. He had an old blanket he had found peeking out of the snow covering the porch swing. He wrapped the filthy wool cloth around himself and sat there, stunned.

The dog rocketed out of the house, moving fast, and disappeared amidst the trees. The blaze grew, but the old woman never came out, and Matthews never heard her scream.

Black smoke billowed upwards into a white sky. After an hour, the blaze was down to a few glowing cinders, as the snow helped to douse the fire, while keeping it from spreading.

Matthews sat on the tree stump and watched it burn, as he enjoyed the warmth. The warmth had been accompanied by a sickening odor, but he tried not to think about that.

The old woman must have been insane to sic the dog on him for no reason, and then, to try to shoot him without cause. Insane, just stark raving mad.

Matthews wandered off into the storm again with the threadbare blanket covering him. If he could find one house, maybe he could find another.

Whenever he thought about the roast chicken, he cried.

22
STORM'S END

When dawn arrived in Siberia, the snow was still falling, but the sun was breaking through the clouds as well.

Inside one of the ruined buildings where Tanner had salvaged wood, a figure stirred. It was a man. He was covered by snow and his face was blackened from frostbite, while a scarlet wound was visible across his scalp.

Nikolai rose from the snow and looked around at a world turned white. There was madness in his eyes, eyes that sat above a ruined nose and lips that had lost circulation during the night. Inside his boots were dead toes and the fingers of his left hand were a bluish-black.

Something caught Nikolai's attention. He watched as a puff of smoke wafted into the air in the near distance. The smoke was coming from Tanner's quinzee.

"I found him. I found Tanner," Nikolai said, but the words pushed out past his dead lips were unintelligible.

His right hand still had some feeling in it. It was gripped around his Serbu shotgun and had been covered by his body during the night. His body's core temperature was at a precariously low level, but Nikolai was beyond feeling the cold. In his madness, he had but one desire—Kill Tanner!

Although his left hand had no feeling, the arm worked. Nikolai bent down, shoved his arm under his companion and pulled her up from beneath the snow. It was Liliya, long since dead and with half her head gone.

"Liliya, I'll show you that I'm better than Fedor. Dozens of men have tried to kill Tanner, but I'll be the one to do it." Again, his words were strange sounds pushed through dead flesh.

Nikolai hobbled through the thigh deep snow while dragging Liliya's body along and looking like something from a demon's daydream. As he neared the hole where the smoke was drifting out, Nikolai, with great care, lowered Liliya's corpse against a tree.

"Wait here where it's safe and I'll be right back."

Nikolai shuffled through the snow and saw that there was an opening at the front of the igloo-like structure. As he moved closer, he thought he heard the faint sound of voices. One of the voices sounded young. Some part of his brain recalled that Tanner had been traveling with a woman and child, but Nikolai was too far gone to care.

Unable to grip the shotgun with more than one hand, Nikolai simply rested the weapon's short barrel against the top of the quinzee and watched as it sank into white powder. The rifle met resistance when it touched the packed snow that comprised the shelter's roof, and Nikolai squeezed the trigger.

Nothing happened. The trigger on the gun was coated with ice. Nikolai pulled harder, grunted, and was rewarded by the first of three blasts.

When Polina screamed in terror after the sound of the first shot, Nikolai cried out in pleasure as he continued to fire. "I got him, Liliya! Honey, I killed him." Nikolai staggered back to Liliya's dead form and plopped down beside it in the snow. "I killed him, Liliya. I killed Tanner. I killed Tanner… and I love you."

Tanner left the quinzee by leaping out and clearing the entrance by ten feet. He had been careful not to land on his injured arm, but the impact with the snow caused it to throb anyway. No one fired at him, and there was no one to fire at, as he had expected.

As he told Sara and Polina the day before, they would build their shelter with defense in mind. They did so, and built a decoy shelter.

Tanner and Polina constructed two quinzees on either side of the natural mound Tanner had chosen as a windbreak. The real quinzee was hollowed out enough to fit them, while the other only had a shallow depression dug out of it.

Above the cavity where the fire burned, a channel was made within the top layer of the two structures, which connected them. But only the false quinzee had a hole in its roof to vent the smoke. Anyone approaching from the old ruins would have seen the smoke, the false opening, and jumped to the wrong conclusion. Nikolai had certainly fallen for the ruse. His first blast had frightened Polina, who'd screamed, and given Tanner time to grab a weapon.

Tanner found Nikolai where he last settled, next to the corpse of Liliya. Nikolai was dead as well, having died seconds earlier. Even in death the madness in Nikolai's eyes was noticeable. Tanner left them there and returned to the quinzee to relay what and who he'd found.

"He fell for our trick," Polina said.

Tanner thought back on the little interaction he'd had with Nikolai. Liliya had clearly been with Fedor, and yet, Nikolai had referred to her as his wife, and he could not let her go even after she'd died.

"He fell very hard," Tanner said.

They headed back toward the city later than they'd planned to, but the bright sun warmed them, while the clear sky was a beautiful sight. Despite the thirty inches of fresh snow they were forced to slog through, and Tanner and Sara's injuries, they were all in good spirits.

Sara was riding on a crude sled made from wood taken from the old structures. She had a rifle in her hands and kept watch for movement while Tanner pulled the sled and Polina struggled along beside him.

Polina wasn't a short girl, but at times, the snowdrifts reached above her waist. Tanner suggested to her that she walk in his wake, but she wanted to stay at his side. That lasted only a short while, then, aware that she was wearing herself out unnecessarily, Polina began following behind Sara's sled.

It was Tanner that spotted him first, then Sara.

They were grateful that Polina had been looking the other way, where a dog, a German shepherd mix, was bounding through the snow, with a freshly caught rabbit in his jaws.

It was Dan Matthews. He was sitting beneath a tree and was huddled inside an old blanket to keep warm. The effort had failed. He was dead. Matthews' open eyes saw nothing, and he was covered with a thin glaze of ice.

The sight pleased Tanner. It saved him the trouble of having to kill the bastard himself.

23
A CASE OF MISTAKEN IDENTITY

VALENTINA AND TWO MEN WERE AT THE LAKE WHERE PAVEL had called from the day before.

When Pavel failed to make contact again, Valentina became worried and decided to go look for him. She knew there was a pit in the area that had acted as a prison for the girl, Polina, and she sent one of the men to look for it. After finding the pit, the man, Ruslan, told her what he'd found, which was nothing.

"The pit is empty?" Valentina asked.

"There is a tent down there," Ruslan said. "And a toilet inside the tent that sits over a hole."

"And no sign of Pavel?"

"No, Valentina, I am sorry. But this is Pavel we're discussing. He must be all right."

"We need to find him. He will have answers."

Ruslan looked at the other man, who was named Bogdan, and saw that Bogdan was thinking the same thing he was. They had been roused out of bed before dawn and fought their way through the final remnants of the snowstorm. They were revolutionaries, yes, but Bogdan made his living as a plumber while Ruslan was a mortician's assistant.

They were tired, hungry, and if the truth be known, scared. Pavel was the muscle of their group. If he had been bested, what chance did they have?

"Valentina," Bogdan said. "Maybe we should go back to the city and wait to hear from Pavel."

"No, we go on and we find him. What if he's injured? We'll start along the ridge. Pavel said he was looking down on the group from there."

"Yes, Valentina," Bogdan said, then he sent a shrug toward Ruslan. Soon, they were back on their snowmobiles and headed along the ridge.

A SHORT TIME LATER, SASHA'S YOUNG NIECE, BRENDA, HAD found the bodies of the wolves and the snow-covered tips of the planes sticking out of the ice, by following in the trail left behind by Valentina. Before leaving to search that morning, Sasha had been advised that there were more people missing, including two local businessmen, Gleb and Aleksandr Dumonovsky.

"We found the planes," Sasha said. "But I don't know why the ice would have cracked like that."

They were keeping back, as the ice near the planes sloped downward toward the large hole in the ice.

There were no bodies left to view. A bear had dragged one away, while the rest had slid into the hole over time, as the aperture dipped lower from the weight of the fresh snow.

"How many men did they say were on those planes?" Durand asked.

"About two dozen, and there's a woman missing too."

The walkie-talkie in Sasha's pocket went off. It was Brenda. She had discovered something else on shore. A few minutes later, Durand was staring down into the pit, which had been left uncovered.

Sasha looked at him. "What the hell is going on, Jacques? It looks like somebody was living down there."

"Or perhaps held captive," Durand said.

Durand climbed down the rope ladder and looked around. He found the remnants of an MRE, and several shoe prints on the mattress. Some were small and appeared to belong to a girl. When he stepped on the metal object, he thought it was a rock. However, after picking it up with a gloved hand and wiping it off, he saw that it was a brass ring. No, not a ring, but more like a tie clip that one might use to keep a bandana tied together. It had an insignia on it that Durand didn't recognize, but Sasha did.

"That belonged to a Girl Scout. I used to have one something like that."

"A Girl Scout? I wasn't aware they were in Russia."

"Oh yeah, and it was a lot of fun too."

Durand wrapped the ring in a tissue and stuck it in his pocket. "Will the search planes be out today?" he asked Sasha.

"Yeah, once they clear the runways, but a group of four hikers went missing west of here, all college kids. They'll be a priority."

Durand pointed out at the lake. "Sara and Tanner were here; I can feel it. And that scene on the lake could be Tanner's handiwork."

"The men in those planes weren't the best citizens. Except for the Dumonovsky brothers, the pilots, and the woman, the rest were all bikers."

"I want to keep heading back north from this direction."

"We will, but let the dogs rest a bit. I'm so glad Brenda has that snowmobile. She's breaking a nice trail for us to follow in."

Durand tramped through the snow to look out at the lake again. Brenda was there and sitting astride her snowmobile.

"Those planes will never fly again," Brenda said.

"Neither will the pilots," Durand said.

"What's that, Jacques?"

"Nothing, I was just thinking out loud."

The whine of two snowmobiles came from their right and soon the machines were visible. The men riding on them were big, young, and tough-looking, but their wool hats and goggles prevented Durand from getting a good look at their faces. The men drove past slowly while studying Brenda and Durand. When they stopped some distance away and spoke to each other, Durand wondered what they were doing.

"That was odd," Brenda said. "And look, they're coming back."

Durand had been a cop for most of his life and had developed certain instincts concerning danger. He had a gun on his hip, and he yanked up the layers of clothing he was wearing so the weapon would be easier to grab.

"Brenda, why don't you go see if Sasha is ready to leave."

"Don't worry, Jacques. She'll ride over when she's ready."

Durand had wanted Brenda away from the men, but it was too late for that anyway. They pulled up to the shore, one on either side of Durand. The thicker of the two spoke to Durand in Russian, but with a middle-eastern accent.

"Are you, Pavel? And is this the package?"

As the man asked that last question, he was looking at Brenda.

The other man pointed at her. "She is not blonde enough and looks older than fourteen."

Brenda appeared to be offended and confused at the same time.

Durand wasn't certain he knew what was happening, but he decided to try to bluff his way through it.

"I am Pavel, but this is not the girl," he said, and although he tried to hide his French accent, it was there and unmistakable.

The thick man hung his head, glanced at his partner, then gave Durand a sour look. "You are not Pavel." The man was bringing a gun out from beneath his jacket when Durand shot him in the face.

Brenda screamed, lost her balance, and fell sideways off her snowmobile, as Durand took aim at the other man.

Durand and the other man fired at each other. Durand's single shot, fired from a Glock, hit the man in the chest. Durand was struck in the chest as well, but with a three-round burst from a Beretta 93R.

Brenda screamed again as Durand fell onto the edge of the lake. When he didn't move, she just knew he was dead.

24

SIGNS OF LIFE

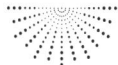

He was dead.

Pavel was dead.

Bogdan and Ruslan stood nearby with sympathetic expressions showing as Valentina wept over her brother's frozen remains.

When she had composed herself, Valentina had them split up and look for tracks in the snow. She found the tracks herself, along with another disturbing scene. There was a dead man who looked like the storm had killed him, but the woman beside him was a mess. She had been bitten by an animal many times, but also shot in the head.

Ruslan, the mortician's assistant, checked them for anything of value, or a clue to their identities. The woman had nothing on her, but the man had been named Nikolai and carried a pilot's license. Ruslan claimed Nikolai's shotgun for his own, although it was empty of shells.

Not far from the bodies was a shelter, cleverly hidden, with tracks leading away from it.

Valentina climbed aboard her snowmobile with a

determined look. She led the way as she followed the path through the snow left behind by Tanner, Sara, and Polina.

When Tanner spotted a patch of space under a huge pine tree that was only sparsely covered with snow, he pulled the sled over to take a break. They had been going for hours and his dislocated arm was killing him, but he was certain they'd be spotted soon or reach a town.

Sara suggested that Tanner and Polina eat something since they were expending so much energy. Tanner declined food, but started a small fire so they could have some tea. He missed coffee, but the MRE only had tea, and he was thankful for that.

Polina was in a good mood, but she was tired of eating food from the MRE's. She had been telling Tanner and Sara about her family, including her grandmother.

Thinking it was a good idea that she should eat something, Tanner offered her some of the beef jerky he found in the tent the Turks had. Polina said she loved beef jerky. It had been a favorite snack food of her chauffeur, Stas, and he had often shared some with her.

After starting the tea, Tanner had taken out a cell phone and tried to get a signal. There was none. He walked up a hill to try again and saw something in the distance that perplexed him. The snow over there was flying about as if driven by a whirlwind and moving in a straight line. When the whirlwind curved some and he saw the black wedge at its front, Tanner realized what it was.

"A train?" Sara said. "That's a good sign."

"It's better than good. That train was a plow clearing the tracks of snow. Once we're rested, I'll cut across these fields and follow those tracks. We'll either get picked up at a road crossing or find a train station."

Sara sighed. "Oh, to soak in a nice hot sudsy bath, and to sleep in a bed again. That will be heaven."

"It might be a hospital bed with that knee of yours."

"I don't think it needs surgery, at least I hope not."

"Tanner."

"Yes, Polina?"

"You never told us what happened to the girl, Genevieve."

"She lived happily ever after."

Sara slapped him on his good arm. "Don't be like that. Tell us the story. You left us in suspense."

"You really want to hear more about that?"

"Yes!" Sara and Polina shouted.

Tanner drained the last of his tea. Then he picked up the story where he'd left off.

25

TANNER AT TWELVE

Cody and his grandfather had returned from another day of hunting. Genevieve came over to talk with him, as Cody was watching the men refuel the plane for the next day. Genevieve had sat out that day's hunt, and Cody expected her to call him more names again, but Genevieve had come to talk for a different reason.

"I'm sorry I called you a monster, Cody. It just scared me to see all that blood… and the guts, yuck."

Cody smiled. He was glad Genevieve wasn't mad at him, and he spotted an opportunity to spend more time with her.

"My granddad is having dinner with your mom in the dining room tonight. Why don't I come by your room?"

Genevieve smiled as she considered Cody. "You want to hang out with me, just the two of us?"

"Uh-huh."

Genevieve laughed. "Are you sure you're only twelve?"

"That's what they tell me, and anyway, you don't want to eat alone, do you?"

"You win, Cody. Come by the room at six and I'll order up a pizza or something."

Cody looked her up and down. "I can't wait."

Genevieve smiled. "I'd better stop thinking of you as a little boy."

CODY'S GRANDFATHER LEFT FOR HIS DINNER DATE WITH Genevieve's mother and Cody raced down two flights of stairs to reach Genevieve's room. The building sat among rolling hills and had been built against a sloping landscape.

Although Genevieve's room was on the second floor, the windows gave a view of snow-covered slopes that some of the guests liked to ski down on occasion. Because of the incline, Genevieve's windows faced a hill.

As he left the stairwell, Cody heard a scream, or rather, a partial scream, because it sounded as if it had been cut off. The hallway outside Genevieve's room was empty, but the entrance to her room was opened a crack, allowing a look inside. Cody called her name as he pushed the door inward.

"Genevieve?"

He saw her through an open window, and she was not alone. A man had her. She was in the man's arms and as limp as a rag doll. The man slipped and fell on his rear in the sloping snow but held on to Genevieve. After he stood, he was moving well again. The man headed toward a pickup truck as he carried Genevieve.

Cody delayed for a moment, as he thought of going for his grandfather, or his rifle, but then he climbed out the window, dropped to the ground, and took off into the night. The pickup truck was silver and looked like the ones they had at the ranch where he lived. His father bought Chevys, and so Cody reasoned that the truck was a Chevy, but this one had those special tires that were made to handle heavy snow.

The pickup fishtailed a bit as the man drove off with Genevieve, but Cody stayed behind it and ran as fast as he could. When the truck reached the parking area, it was illuminated by the lights coming from the dining room windows. Cody hoped that his grandfather, Genevieve's mom, or someone would wonder why a truck would have been up on that hill.

Once the vehicle was on asphalt, Cody fell behind quickly, and he stopped running as he reached the end of the driveway. Many boys would have been crying in frustration or fear, but Cody Parker was thinking. He had stopped running because it was futile to chase after the truck on foot, and he knew he needed a better plan.

It came to him as he imagined the terrain. He had seen the area surrounding the ranch when he and his grandfather arrived, and just that morning too, when they had gone into town for breakfast.

The truck with Genevieve in it would have to navigate down a series of long winding curves. Those curves not only wound, but they were icy as well. The man would have to slow, would have to take his time or risk having an accident, and when he reached the bottom, he'd be directly below.

Cody walked over to the edge of the driveway, where the asphalt ended, and looked down a snow-covered slope of land that went on for over a mile. There was a moon above that wasn't full, but was bright enough to give light as it reflected off the snow.

Cody made his mind up and started down the hill.

Within a hundred yards he was sliding along on his backside and picking up speed.

When he feared he was going too fast, he tried to slow himself. That effort resulted in turning him around, and then he was sliding backwards. He hit a small tree, just a glancing blow on a shoulder, and it spun him around a turn and a half. He was facing the right way again, but it gave him no pleasure, because up ahead was blackness.

Cody sailed off into the night while making an "ooh" sound, as a tremor of fear passed through him, one that was accompanied by a greater rush of excitement.

It felt like he had been falling forever when he landed hard on the branch of a pine tree. The branch gave way, dipped, then sprang back up, and he was flung through the air again. He landed on his back in deep snow with his knees slightly bent, then felt himself sliding backwards again. A grab at a bush halted his slide and he stood.

He was good, other than a few sore spots and a deep scratch on the back of his neck. When he gazed upward, he was amazed at how far he had come down. The roadway was a hundred yards away. Cody half ran, half slid the rest of the way down. When he stepped into the road, he saw the pickup on his left. It was exiting the road that led to the lodge and headed south.

Cody ran straight ahead, where the land was cleared and mostly flat. The road going south curved, and if he could just run fast enough, he might meet the truck on the other side of the clearing. When he was halfway across the field, Cody knew he'd been far too optimistic, as the truck went by out on the road. Still, it was the only vehicle in sight. Cody kept running, with his knees rising and falling like twin pistons, and his fists clenched.

When the truck made a left, he was over a mile behind, but could still see its lights. The truck traveled another few seconds, made a right, then, a quick left, and disappeared, or perhaps cut its lights off.

Cody kept running on an angle for the truck. When he saw a vehicle approaching, he thought it was the truck coming back, but no, it was a car. When the car came to the intersection Cody was approaching, he shouted at it. The driver, who had the silhouette of an old man, didn't hear him, and drove off in the other direction.

Cody shivered from the cold. He was wet from his slide down the hill, but he couldn't go back until he found that truck, and Genevieve.

There were headlights coming from behind Cody, from back near the lodge. As he stood still and gulped in air, he thought about running toward them. However, there was no guarantee that the driver wouldn't veer off down another road before he could reach them and ask for help.

Cody ran again and headed toward the last spot he'd seen the truck. As he rounded a curve, he spotted it. The truck was parked in front of an old shack that was at the foot of a hill. It reminded Cody of a supply shed they had on his family's ranch, but this building the man had taken Genevieve to was much older. The slanted roof of the structure looked as if it would let in water, while the windows were coated with dust.

Cody approached the truck in a crouch. The engine was off. When he tried the handle on the passenger side, it was locked. A glance into a side window showed him the vehicle was empty.

A noise came from inside, followed by the sound of a man shouting. The door on the shack was weathered and the doorknob was missing. Cody eased it open, heard the man shout again, and could tell that he was at the rear.

Then, the screaming started. It was Genevieve. She

was screaming in hysteria, pleading with the man to let her go, but he answered her by laughing.

"Scream all you want, you little bitch. No one will hear you. Now, let's see what you got under that blouse."

Cody was surprised by the man's voice. He sounded young. He had only seen the man once and from the rear, but the twelve-year-old had always thought that guys who abducted girls were old men, like in their forties.

Cody peeked around the corner and saw the man rip open Genevieve's blouse to expose the white lace bra beneath it. She was standing on her toes with her arms over her head and her wrists tied together by rope.

The man spoke to Genevieve. He described what he would do to her, and when Genevieve wept and moaned in terror, Cody saw the side of the man's face. He was grinning. The bastard was enjoying Genevieve's fear.

Cody claimed a broken 2X4 that was laying on the floor. It was dusty, and there was a nail sticking out of it, a long nail. Cody entered the room as the man gripped Genevieve's bra, preparing to rip it open.

Genevieve saw Cody and her wide eyes wouldn't leave him. When the man looked at her, he followed her gaze, moved to duck, but was too late to prevent getting hit. He had avoided the nail, but not the board. It caught him on the side of the head. The man stumbled backwards, hit a table, and crashed to the floor, where he lay still.

Cody was advancing on him, but Genevieve begged to be freed from the ropes that held her wrists. Cody followed the path of the rope, saw how it went over a wooden beam and down to a crossbar in a wall, where the plaster had rotted away. It was a simple slipknot. Cody pulled it, and Genevieve's arms dropped.

She cried and mumbled something that Cody couldn't

make out as he freed her wrists, while trying not to stare at her breasts.

"Go Genevieve, run outside and hide somewhere."

"What? Come with me."

"I can't," Cody said, as he raised the 2X4 again.

Genevieve looked at the wood, then Cody, then at the man who tried to rape her. She headed out of the room and said she'd get help.

Cody watched her go. When he turned back around, the man punched him in the face, and he hit the floor. The man looked down at him for a moment as Cody stared up. There was surprise on the man's face. He had expected Cody to be out cold. What he didn't know is that Cody was no stranger to fighting. Although he was only twelve, he had learned to box well from a man who worked on his family's ranch.

Cody and the ranch hand sparred often, as the man was short, lean, and boxed in the Flyweight Division, at 112 lbs.

Cody could take a punch all right, and he also knew how to give them. He bounced up from the floor as the man grabbed the 2X4. The man swung at Cody as Cody grabbed for the 2X4 to wrest it away. The nail sticking out of the wood punctured Cody's hand. It hurt like hell and would leave a scar, but when Cody yanked his hand away, the 2X4 came with it and clattered to the floor.

Cody ducked the next punch the man threw, then he hit the man in the stomach with a right. That was followed by a left to the nose. The man backed away from him while grunting. He had fifty pounds and nine inches on the boy standing before him, but the kid had hurt him.

The man charged Cody. Cody hit him with a right cross that rocked the man's head, but the momentum of his charge pushed Cody to the floor. The man straddled

Cody, blocked his punches with one hand, then grabbed up the 2X4 with the other.

Cody struggled to push the man off, but his weight was too much. The man raised the 2X4 high and prepared to bring it crashing down on Cody's skull.

Tanner ended the story there and Sara and Polina stared at him with impatience.

"Well, go on," Sara said. "Tell us what happened next."

Tanner shrugged. "The man bashed my head in and killed me. The end."

Sara punched him playfully in the stomach, but Polina laughed.

"I know what happened," Polina said, as she stood and pantomimed fighting. "Boy Tanner smash man in the nose and beat him up good, then helped the girl and found the police."

"It was something like that," Tanner said.

Polina looked around. "I have to tinkle. I'll be right back."

While Polina was gone, Tanner and Sara cleaned the area and prepared to move out again. When they saw a small plane off in the distance, it gave them both hope that they were nearing civilization.

"We should have been able to get a cell signal by now," Sara said.

"Something must be wrong with the system," Tanner told her. As he spoke, he looked off to where Polina had gone.

Sara realized where he was looking and grew concerned. "She's been gone a while, hasn't she?"

"Yeah."

Sara stood with difficulty. There was less snow beneath the trees, and she used her cane to help her hobble along. Tanner assisted her as they reached the top of the small hill, and they saw Polina, who was not alone.

There was a wolf there. It was *the* wolf, and it was growling as it approached Polina.

26

VIVE LA REVOLUTION—NOT!

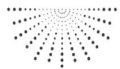

"I just knew you were dead."

Jacques Durand smiled at Sasha's pretty niece, Brenda. "I might be dead if I hadn't worn my bulletproof vest for extra warmth."

Durand was sipping on coffee near a fire. They were still at the lake, but had been joined by local police and a paramedic. One of the locals deep in the woods had made it into town on his own dog sled and reported hearing lots of gunfire the day before, along with a woman's screams.

When Brenda took off to get help, she ran into the cop riding a snowmobile. The cop had found the bodies of Gleb and Aleksandr and had already requested backup. When he saw the planes in the lake, the men Durand had shot, and the wounded Durand, he called everybody.

Durand's wounds consisted of three nasty bruises on his chest and a bump on the head. He had hit the lake ice hard as he went down and banged his forehead. The man he'd shot in the face was dead, but his partner survived, and was said to be asking for a deal.

Sasha walked over, kissed Durand on the cheek, then

hugged him. "Thank you for saving Brenda from those men."

"You're welcome, but I don't think they were after her. There's something else going on here."

There was a flurry of activity out on the lake. There was a helicopter there. Snow had been shoved aside by the police to make a space for the craft to land, and the chopper had brought in a team of crime scene investigators. One of the men ran toward Durand.

When he was closer, Durand saw that he was holding up a clear plastic baggie with the brass tie ring Durand had found earlier. He had given it to the crime scene people when they arrived and pointed them toward the pit.

"Sir, you say you found this in the pit?"

"Yes, why?"

"It might be nothing, but the Nabokov girl, the kidnap victim, she was wearing her Girl Scout uniform when she was abducted."

"Not blonde enough and looks older than fourteen," Durand said, as he repeated what one of his attackers had said earlier.

"What was that?" the cop asked.

"Your kidnap victim, is she blonde and fourteen?"

"Yes."

"The men I shot. They had come here to get her, and they almost mistook Brenda for her."

The cop holding the tie clasp smiled. "I think we just got a break."

VALENTINA KICKED DAN MATTHEWS' CORPSE IN THE FACE and watched it fall over. She was frustrated because she was being delayed in her pursuit of Pavel's killer. They'd had been following the trail left behind by Tanner, Sara, and Polina when they came to the tree.

It was a massive cedar. The tree's root ball had come loose from the ground after being unable to bear the weight of the ice and snow coating it. The fallen tree was too high to get over and the hills on either side were too steep for the snowmobiles. Bogdan had tried and damaged a ski on his machine. He could fix it, but it took time. Once that was done, they would still need to backtrack to get around the tree.

Ruslan walked over. He liked Valentina and thought she was beautiful, but never dared to ask her out.

The Revolution was everything to the woman, and although Ruslan believed in the cause, he found her fanaticism intimidating.

"Who do you think this man was?" Ruslan asked.

"One of the bastards who took the girl. The others must have kicked him out of the shelter, or else he became lost."

"Bogdan is almost finished with his repair, then we can be on our way."

Valentina turned to look at Ruslan. "We will kill these people when we find them."

Ruslan blinked fast several times. "Da. I am armed, and I'm ready to do what you need me to do."

"Good," Valentina said, and the briefest of smiles appeared on her lips.

Ruslan looked at her as she went to speak with Bogdan. He would kill. If it made Valentina happy, he would kill hundreds. He followed behind her, watching the sway of her hips, while daydreaming about nights that would never come.

∼

Sara had left the rifle back at the sled, but Tanner had a handgun. The wolf had yet to notice them, as he was focused on Polina. The wolf was a big one, with a weight approaching a hundred pounds.

Polina appeared calm and Tanner was impressed with her once more. As he brought the gun up to take aim, he saw Polina reach for something in her pocket.

"Oh no, Tanner. She's reaching for her knife," Sara said.

But it wasn't a knife. It was half a stick of the beef jerky Tanner had given her. Polina took the food from its wrapper, held it up, then, she tossed the beef jerky at the wolf.

The animal followed its path and watched it fall in front of him, to sink down in the snow. After sniffing the air, the wolf stepped forward and plucked the food from the frost. He chewed, swallowed, then stared back at Polina.

She showed the wolf her empty hands and spoke to it in Russian. "I have no more. I am sorry."

The wolf stared at her for several seconds. When it lifted its leg to move, Tanner almost fired, but the wolf turned and ran off into the trees a dozen yards away.

"Polina," Tanner called.

She ran to them with joy lighting her face. "Did you two see the wolf?"

"Yes, and that beast is dangerous," Sara said.

Polina shook her head. "Only to the bad people."

Tanner helped Sara down the hill and onto the sled. It took a while, but they reached the railroad tracks. The railway plow had done a fine job. It had scattered the snow from off the tracks and several feet to each side of them. Sara gave up the makeshift sled and began walking.

"Are you sure your knee feels good enough?" Tanner asked.

"If we go slow and I use the cane, but how's your arm?"

"It feels like it's on fire, but I'll be fine."

They rounded a curve in the tracks and saw a metal tower far off in the distance.

"A cell tower!" Sara said with a smile.

"Let's see," Tanner said. He took out his phone and saw two bars appear. "We have service again."

"Look!" Polina said, and she pointed the way they had come, where three snowmobiles were following in the tracks made by the sled.

Tanner put the phone away as the snowmobiles' whining engines came into hearing range. The three snowmobiles left their sight as they joined up with the railroad tracks, but within moments, they were coming around the curve, then cut their engines.

Tanner eyed the three riders with suspicion, as did Sara, but when the one in the middle removed her goggles and helmet. Polina lit up in a smile and ran to her.

"Miss Krasotkin! It's Miss Krasotkin; she's one of my teachers."

The woman got off the snowmobile and greeted Polina with a hug. "Polina! What are you doing here?"

As the woman spoke, the men got off their machines.

"Miss Krasotkin, these are my friends, Sara and Tanner. They are Americans and they saved me."

"Saved you from what, dear?"

"I was kidnapped by a man when I left school Friday."

Valentina Krasotkin pretended to look astonished as she straightened up. "Kidnapped?"

"Polina was kidnapped two days ago. You hadn't heard?" Tanner said.

"Why no, I was at home with a cold. Oh, my goodness, thank God you found her."

Tanner quickly explained in English what Valentina had said in Russian. He saw that Sara understood the significance. While there might be differences in the way Russian and American authorities handled a high-level kidnapping, the Russian authorities certainly would have tracked down and talked to anyone Polina knew. Valentina's professed ignorance was a lie.

One man went to Tanner's left, that was Bogdan, who had seen Tanner's injured arm hanging in the sling and sought to take advantage of the ailment. Meanwhile, Ruslan was on Tanner's right.

Ruslan had a hand hidden behind his leg, and the hand was holding something. Tanner was wondering if Sara was aware of the threat when she whispered to him.

"I have the one on the left," Sara said.

Tanner's gun was out in a flash and firing at Ruslan.

Ruslan's front teeth shattered as Tanner's bullet passed through them on its way out the rear of the man's skull. Before Ruslan's body had even hit the ground, Tanner had spun and shot Bogdan, who had already suffered a fatal head wound delivered by Sara.

Polina screamed in shock, then was yanked in front of Valentina, who attempted to use the girl as a shield. She pointed her gun at Polina.

"I'll kill her if you don't drop those weapons."

Tanner and Sara ignored her. How would giving up their only means of defense help Polina in the slightest?

Tanner was taking careful aim at a spot on Valentina's forehead when Polina surprised all of them. With a shout, she grabbed Valentina's sleeve, shifted her hips, and flipped the woman sideways.

Valentina fell hard onto the metal tracks and cried out

in pain. She then sat up, but before she could raise her weapon, Sara smashed her cane against the crown of Valentina's head. The cane broke, and Valentina fell back over.

Polina ran to Tanner, and he put his good arm around her shoulders. "Who taught you how to do a hip flip, was it your chauffeur, Stas?"

Polina opened her jacket, pulled up the layers beneath, and pointed at one of the patches on her uniform blouse.

"Self-defense classes; I learned at the Girl Scouts."

As Polina helped Tanner bind Valentina's wrists and ankles together, the woman stirred awake. When she saw that she was captured, Valentina cried, then begged Tanner to kill her.

"You must kill me," she told Tanner.

"Why?"

"I am not a criminal. I am a revolutionary, a soldier, I should not be taken alive."

"I don't care about your politics," Tanner said. "I only care that you and your people hurt Polina."

Valentina gazed at Tanner with a look of hatred. "Did you kill Pavel?"

"I did, but I won't kill you. I'll let the authorities have you. Once they make you talk, your people won't be kidnapping any more girls."

"Pavel was my brother. I'll see you dead one day."

Tanner considered Valentina. Perhaps it would be best to kill her. But no, if she were part of a conspiracy, there were people in the Russian government that would make her talk. That information could prove invaluable.

Sara's phone rang.

She laughed with delight as she dug it out and answered it with a smile in her voice. "Hello, Jacques."

"Sara! Thank God. Are you safe?"

"I am and so is Tanner."

"Nothing can kill that man. It's you I was worried about."

"Thank you, and I have hurt my knee, but Tanner needs a doctor too, for a dislocated elbow."

"Where are you two? I'll come with help."

"You're near?"

"I've been searching for you."

"Thank you, that means a lot to me, but listen, Jacques. We have a girl with us."

"Polina Nabokov."

"How did you know?"

"That's a long story."

"You can tell it to me when you see me," Sara said. She ended the call after talking to a policeman who said he knew the area and that help was on the way. When her phone rang a minute later, the call was for Polina.

Sara handed her the phone and watched the girl fill with happiness at the sound of her mother's voice.

Sara reached over and took Tanner's hand.

"I'd crash all over again if it meant saving Polina."

Tanner said nothing, but there was a smile on his face.

27
HERO?

After rescue teams arrived with the police and federal agents, Durand, with the assistance of Polina's grandmother, covered up Tanner and Sara's involvement in saving Polina from Pavel and the others.

Valentina refused to talk, but the Russian authorities were confident that they could uncover any of the other members of their organization by a detailed examination into the lives of its deceased conspirators, such as Bogdan and Ruslan. And although it wasn't stated, Valentina would likely be tortured to reveal what she knew. Regardless of the level of interrogation she was subjected to, Valentina's remaining days would be spent behind bars.

When it came to Tanner and Sara's involvement, Polina promised she would keep it a secret.

Durand's guide, Sasha, received the reward for finding Polina.

After saying goodbye to Sara at the airport, Polina asked to speak to Tanner in private. They talked in a quiet corner of the airport terminal, where Polina used a black marker to draw something on the white fabric of the splint

Tanner had to wear on his left forearm. The splint resembled a cast, but it was soft and could be flexed. Tanner would be wearing it for at least two weeks while he recovered from the injury he received in his fight with Pavel.

While watching from the other side of the large room, Sara saw Polina give Tanner a quick kiss on the lips, before wiping away tears as they said goodbye.

SARA WORE A KNEE BRACE THAT COMPLEMENTED TANNER'S splint as they headed for the United States.

As their jet left Paris after a brief layover for refueling, Sara asked a question. "What did Polina say before she kissed you?"

Tanner wore a smile. "She said I was her hero."

"Speaking of young girls, whatever happened between you and the girl you met at twelve? You left me in suspense there. But even at twelve, I'm sure you found a way to win."

"Actually, I had help."

CODY WAS PINNED TO THE FLOOR AND STRUGGLING TO GET free, as the man who had abducted Genevieve raised the 2X4 to bash his skull in.

A shot rang out. The bullet whizzed over the man's left shoulder, just missing him. Both the man and Cody turned their heads to see Cody's grandfather holding a gun. The man dropped the 2X4 and put his hands in the air.

Walter Parker stepped closer, took aim, and shot the man in the heart. Genevieve's abductor crumpled backwards, to lie dead on the floor, while Cody got to his feet.

"Are you all right, boy? I saw you two fighting, but I had trouble getting a clean shot."

"I'm good, Granddad. Where's Genevieve?"

"In my truck with her mother. We saw you running through the parking lot without a coat on and couldn't figure out what you were doing. When I went out looking for you, we found Genevieve."

The wound on Cody's hand was bandaged inside an ambulance, while he also had multiple bruises from his tumble down the hill. A blanket was draped over his shoulders, but he was still cold from the damp clothes he was wearing.

When cops questioned him about the shots his grandfather had fired, Cody said that the heart shot came first, and that the second shot missed high. He said nothing about the dead man having raised his hands in surrender. When his grandfather asked him why he lied, Cody answered with a question.

"Would the man have done it again, you know, grab a girl like Genevieve?"

"Yes," his grandfather said, "and that's why I killed him."

"And that's why I lied," Cody said.

His grandfather took him by the shoulders and stared at him with pride. "You nearly fought that bastard to a standstill, at only twelve. You'll make a hell of a man someday, boy. Yes sir, one hell of a man."

Sara leaned over and kissed Tanner. "Polina was right, you are a hero… in a way."

"I'm a hit man, not a hero," Tanner said, then he drifted off into thoughts about the past again.

Genevieve had come to the door and asked to talk to Cody before she left the lodge with her mother. His grandfather said that they could talk while he went down to the lobby to buy pipe tobacco. Cody realized the old man was giving them time alone, and he loved him for it.

While his grandfather was gone, Genevieve gave Cody her phone number, along with an embrace and a long kiss on the lips.

"You're my hero, Cody Parker, and I'll never forget you."

Tanner didn't know if, wherever she was, Genevieve still remembered him or not, but he knew he'd never forget her kiss, it had been his first.

Tanner looked at his left palm, where a wound from an ancient battle left a faded white scar he would always carry. Above that hand, there was a heart drawn on his splint. Polina had written her name along with the words, "I love you," in the Cyrillic script used in Russia.

"That girl, Genevieve, did you two stay in touch?" Sara asked.

"After two phone calls, I realized we had nothing to say to each other and that she was just being nice. I never called again."

Sara pointed at the heart Polina drew. "Genevieve gave

you her phone number, and years later, you're still winning young girls' hearts."

Tanner stared into Sara's eyes. "And what about big girls?"

Sara kissed him. "Oh yeah, you've got my heart."

Before they could say more, Sara was overcome by a yawn. She stretched, then reclined her seat.

"I need sleep, but wake me before we land."

"Will do," Tanner said.

They were headed for New York City, and it would be so good to be back home.

TANNER RETURNS!

MANHATTAN HIT MAN - BOOK 18

AFTERWORD

Thank you,

REMINGTON KANE

JOIN MY INNER CIRCLE

You'll receive FREE books, such as,

SLAY BELLS – A TANNER NOVEL – BOOK 0

TAKEN! ALPHABET SERIES – 26 ORIGINAL TAKEN! TALES

BLUE STEELE - KARMA

Also – Exclusive short stories featuring TANNER, along with other books.

TO BECOME AN INNER CIRCLE MEMBER, GO TO:
http://remingtonkane.com/mailing-list/

ALSO BY REMINGTON KANE

The TANNER Series in order

INEVITABLE I - A Tanner Novel - Book 1

KILL IN PLAIN SIGHT - A Tanner Novel - Book 2

MAKING A KILLING ON WALL STREET - A Tanner Novel - Book 3

THE FIRST ONE TO DIE LOSES - A Tanner Novel - Book 4

THE LIFE & DEATH OF CODY PARKER - A Tanner Novel - Book 5

WAR - A Tanner Novel- A Tanner Novel - Book 6

SUICIDE OR DEATH - A Tanner Novel - Book 7

TWO FOR THE KILL - A Tanner Novel - Book 8

BALLET OF DEATH - A Tanner Novel - Book 9

MORE DANGEROUS THAN MAN - A Tanner Novel - Book 10

TANNER TIMES TWO - A Tanner Novel - Book 11

OCCUPATION: DEATH - A Tanner Novel - Book 12

HELL FOR HIRE - A Tanner Novel - Book 13

A HOME TO DIE FOR - A Tanner Novel - Book 14

FIRE WITH FIRE - A Tanner Novel - Book 15

TO KILL A KILLER - A Tanner Novel - Book 16

WHITE HELL – A Tanner Novel - Book 17

MANHATTAN HIT MAN – A Tanner Novel - Book 18

ONE HUNDRED YEARS OF TANNER – A Tanner Novel -

Book 19

REVELATIONS - A Tanner Novel - Book 20

THE SPY GAME - A Tanner Novel - Book 21

A VICTIM OF CIRCUMSTANCE - A Tanner Novel - Book 22

A MAN OF RESPECT - A Tanner Novel - Book 23

THE MAN, THE MYTH - A Tanner Novel - Book 24

ALL-OUT WAR - A Tanner Novel - Book 25

THE REAL DEAL - A Tanner Novel - Book 26

WAR ZONE - A Tanner Novel - Book 27

ULTIMATE ASSASSIN - A Tanner Novel - Book 28

KNIGHT TIME - A Tanner Novel - Book 29

PROTECTOR - A Tanner Novel - Book 30

BULLETS BEFORE BREAKFAST - A Tanner Novel - Book 31

VENGEANCE - A Tanner Novel - Book 32

TARGET: TANNER - A Tanner Novel - Book 33

BLACK SHEEP - A Tanner Novel - Book 34

FLESH AND BLOOD - A Tanner Novel - Book 35

NEVER SEE IT COMING - A Tanner Novel - Book 36

MISSING - A Tanner Novel - Book 37

CONTENDER - A Tanner Novel - Book 38

TO SERVE AND PROTECT - A Tanner Novel - Book 39

STALKING HORSE - A Tanner Novel - Book 40

THE EVIL OF TWO LESSERS - A Tanner Novel - Book 41

SINS OF THE FATHER AND MOTHER - A Tanner Novel - Book 42

SOULLESS - A Tanner Novel - Book 43

The Young Guns Series in order

YOUNG GUNS

YOUNG GUNS 2 - SMOKE & MIRRORS

YOUNG GUNS 3 - BEYOND LIMITS

YOUNG GUNS 4 - RYKER'S RAIDERS

YOUNG GUNS 5 - ULTIMATE TRAINING

YOUNG GUNS 6 - CONTRACT TO KILL

YOUNG GUNS 7 - FIRST LOVE

YOUNG GUNS 8 - THE END OF THE BEGINNING

A Tanner Series in order

TANNER: YEAR ONE

TANNER: YEAR TWO

TANNER: YEAR THREE

TANNER: YEAR FOUR

TANNER: YEAR FIVE

The TAKEN! Series in order

TAKEN! - LOVE CONQUERS ALL - Book 1

TAKEN! - SECRETS & LIES - Book 2

TAKEN! - STALKER - Book 3

TAKEN! - BREAKOUT! - Book 4

TAKEN! - THE THIRTY-NINE - Book 5

TAKEN! - KIDNAPPING THE DEVIL - Book 6

TAKEN! - HIT SQUAD - Book 7

TAKEN! - MASQUERADE - Book 8

TAKEN! - SERIOUS BUSINESS - Book 9

TAKEN! - THE COUPLE THAT SLAYS TOGETHER - Book 10

TAKEN! - PUT ASUNDER - Book 11

TAKEN! - LIKE BOND, ONLY BETTER - Book 12

TAKEN! - MEDIEVAL - Book 13

TAKEN! - RISEN! - Book 14

TAKEN! - VACATION - Book 15

TAKEN! - MICHAEL - Book 16

TAKEN! - BEDEVILED - Book 17

TAKEN! - INTENTIONAL ACTS OF VIOLENCE - Book 18

TAKEN! - THE KING OF KILLERS – Book 19

TAKEN! - NO MORE MR. NICE GUY - Book 20 & the Series Finale

The MR. WHITE Series

PAST IMPERFECT - MR. WHITE - Book 1

HUNTED - MR. WHITE - Book 2

The BLUE STEELE Series in order

BLUE STEELE - BOUNTY HUNTER- Book 1

BLUE STEELE - BROKEN- Book 2

BLUE STEELE - VENGEANCE- Book 3

BLUE STEELE - THAT WHICH DOESN'T KILL ME- Book 4

BLUE STEELE - ON THE HUNT- Book 5

BLUE STEELE - PAST SINS - Book 6

BLUE STEELE - DADDY'S GIRL - Book 7 & the Series Finale

The CALIBER DETECTIVE AGENCY Series in order

CALIBER DETECTIVE AGENCY - GENERATIONS- Book 1

CALIBER DETECTIVE AGENCY - TEMPTATION- Book 2

CALIBER DETECTIVE AGENCY - A RANSOM PAID IN BLOOD- Book 3

CALIBER DETECTIVE AGENCY - MISSING- Book 4

CALIBER DETECTIVE AGENCY - DECEPTION- Book 5

CALIBER DETECTIVE AGENCY - CRUCIBLE- Book 6

CALIBER DETECTIVE AGENCY – LEGENDARY – Book 7

CALIBER DETECTIVE AGENCY – WE ARE GATHERED HERE TODAY - Book 8

CALIBER DETECTIVE AGENCY - MEANS, MOTIVE, and OPPORTUNITY - Book 9 & the Series Finale

THE TAKEN!/TANNER Series in order

THE CONTRACT: KILL JESSICA WHITE - Taken!/Tanner - Book 1

UNFINISHED BUSINESS – Taken!/Tanner – Book 2

THE ABDUCTION OF THOMAS LAWSON - Taken!/Tanner – Book 3

PREDATOR - Taken!/Tanner - Book 4

DETECTIVE PIERCE Series in order

MONSTERS - A Detective Pierce Novel - Book 1

DEMONS - A Detective Pierce Novel - Book 2

ANGELS - A Detective Pierce Novel - Book 3

THE OCEAN BEACH ISLAND Series in order

THE MANY AND THE ONE - Book 1

SINS & SECOND CHANES - Book 2

DRY ADULTERY, WET AMBITION - Book 3

OF TONGUE AND PEN - Book 4

ALL GOOD THINGS… - Book 5

LITTLE WHITE SINS - Book 6

THE LIGHT OF DARKNESS - Book 7

STERN ISLAND - Book 8 & the Series Finale

THE REVENGE Series in order

JOHNNY REVENGE - The Revenge Series - Book 1

THE APPOINTMENT KILLER - The Revenge Series - Book 2

AN I FOR AN I - The Revenge Series - Book 3

ALSO

THE EFFECT: Reality is changing!

THE FIX-IT MAN: A Tale of True Love and Revenge

DOUBLE OR NOTHING

PARKER & KNIGHT

REDEMPTION: Someone's taken her

DESOLATION LAKE

TIME TRAVEL TALES & OTHER SHORT STORIES

WHITE HELL
Copyright © REMINGTON KANE, 2017
YEAR ZERO PUBLISHING

This book is a work of fiction. Names, characters, places and incidents either are products of the author's imagination or are used fictitiously.

Any resemblance to actual events or locales or persons, living or dead, is entirely coincidental.

All rights reserved. Except as permitted under the U.S. Copyright Act of 1976, no part of this publication may be reproduced, distributed or transmitted in any form or by any means, or stored in a database or retrieval system, without the prior written permission of the publisher.

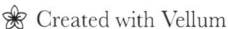 Created with Vellum

Printed in Great Britain
by Amazon